WEERD

Patrick Winters

Copyright © Patrick Winters, 2018

All rights reserved

"Before the Ash," "Old Shuck," and "Damned Happy" first appeared in *Sanitarium Magazine*, copyright © Patrick Winters, 2014, 2017

"Carly's Seventh" first appeared in *The Sirens Call,* copyright © Patrick Winters, 2017

"Goodnight's Alternative Carnival of Curiosities" first appeared in *Massacre Magazine*, copyright © Patrick Winters, 2017

"The Pitch" first appeared on *Literally Stories*, copyright © Patrick Winters, 2017

"Little Bastard" first appeared in *Schlock Magazine*, copyright © Patrick Winters, 2017

"Chirp" first appeared in *Ghostlight, the Magazine of Terror*, edited by Nicole Castle, copyright © Patrick Winters, 2015

"The Time I Done Pranked Some Spacemen" first appeared on *Horror Sleaze Trash,* copyright © Patrick Winters, 2017

"Her Name's Not John" first appeared in *Trysts of Fate*, edited by LA Story Sikora, copyright © Patrick Winters, 2016

"Though He Walks" first appeared in *Deadman's Tome,* edited by Jesse Dedman, copyright © Patrick Winters, 2017

Cover art created by Aric Salyer
https://salyeraric.wixsite.com/artist-portfolio

ISBN 978-0-692-10551-1

To all the weird hearts out there—stay weird.

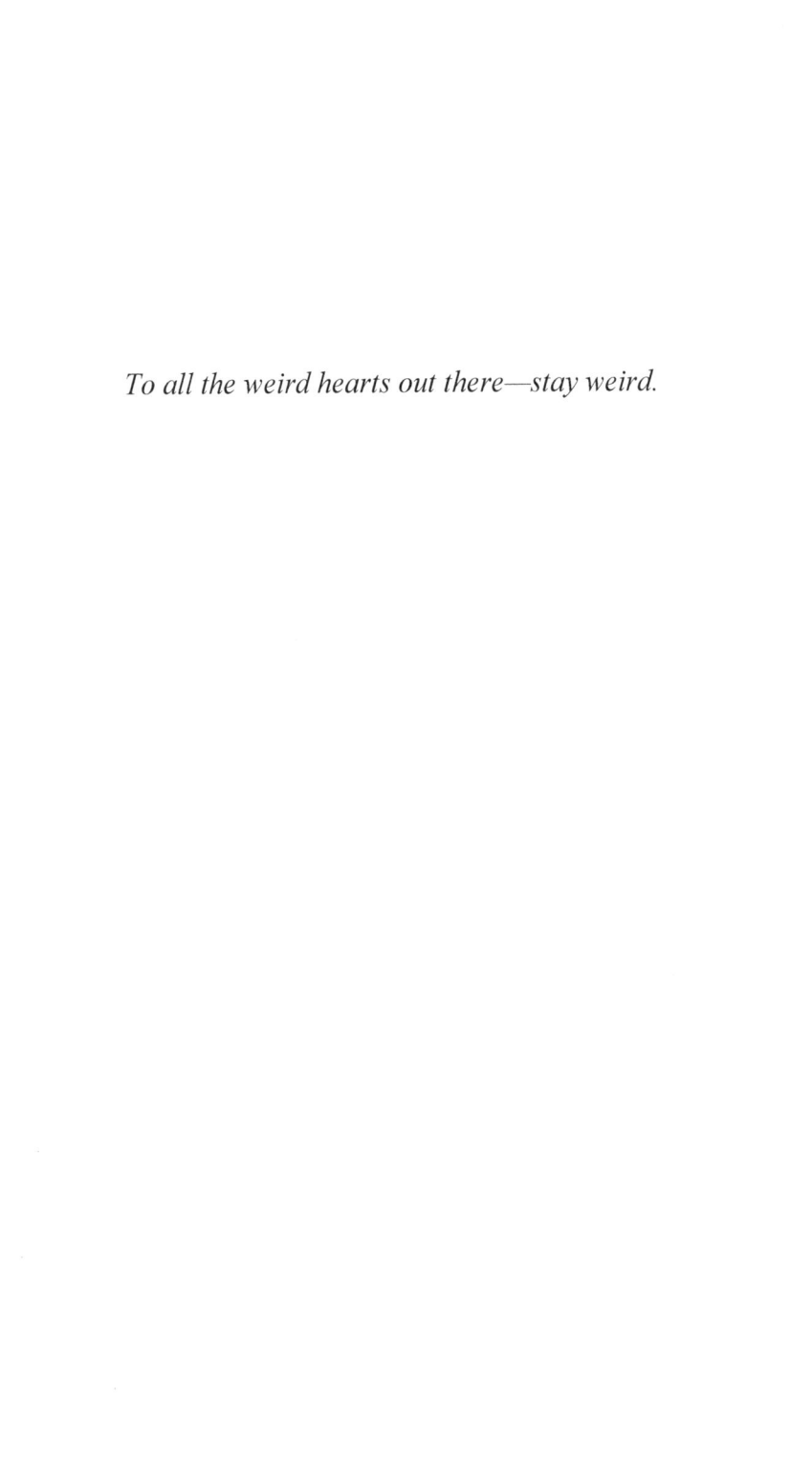

4

Table of Contents

Before the Ash 7

Carly's Seventh 31

Goodnight's Alternative Carnival of Curiosities 43

The Pitch 73

The Four Laddies 87

Little Bastard 111

Chirp 131

Leaving the Lasso 153

Old Shuck 159

Damned Happy 177

Vegas Moon 203

The Time I Done Pranked Some Spacemen 251

Just Another Monday 259

The Puckwudgie, or Thomas Clay and His Convictions ... 271

Her Name's Not John 285

Though He Walks 309

6

Before the Ash

"Ashes to ashes, me to you — Carl Blanch"

The note left with the urn was as brief as it was confounding.

Shawn Dwyer didn't know which was more peculiar: the note, with its cryptic and nonsensical message, or the urn, which had just been left on his desk for him to find at his lunch break's end.

He stood in the mouth of his confined little cubicle now, staring down at both items with confusion and a fair hint of disgust, having slowly backed away from the urn after reading the message scrawled on the piece of paper that was perched on the lid. He'd treated the odd container like it was some kind of bomb, a dangerous and untrustworthy thing that would blow him to Hell the moment he made a wrong move; he felt this was a safer distance from which to analyze the urn.

It hadn't been there an hour ago when he left his desk in the call-center. That was for damn sure. Whoever had left it had to have placed it there while he was gone, out to Subway for his meager meal. But who had left it there? And most importantly, why?

Shawn's mind reeled with a fluster of possibilities. Was it some practical joke, born of some coworker's twisted idea of humor? He surely found no humor in it, if that were the case. Was it some mysterious and symbolic threat against him, a forewarning meant to be unnerving to him, as it proved to be? He had no enemies, as far as he knew. Or so he hoped.

Could it have been some mistake, the urn and its note left at his work station by accident, intended for somebody other than himself? That seemed the most likely—and pleasant—of possibilities.

But as he stared at the urn, looking at the bent and contorted image of himself reflected on its round, golden side, he didn't believe it was a mistake. He had the distinct feeling it was meant for him to find and to have.

Ashes to ashes, me to you — Carl Blanch.

Carl Blanch. Was that meant to be a signature? Shawn could only assume so. He repeated the name over and over again in his mind. It didn't sound at all familiar to him. He tried putting the name to a face, to a coworker or distant family member, to a time or place. But nothing came to him. He was certain he didn't know any Carl Blanch.

Ashes to ashes, me to you.

Shawn shrugged off the chill that tingled over the nape of his neck and turned around, leaving his cubicle. He was determined to get to the bottom of this unwanted mystery. Maybe somebody else in the call-center had some insight as to what this was all about.

Shawn went to Clay Burrows in the cubicle next to his own, asking if Clay had seen anyone at his desk lately. Clay said he hadn't, that he'd just returned from his own lunch break a few minutes before. Shawn thanked him and moved to the other workers in the immediate area—the ones that he thought would be honest and trustworthy. After questioning them, each said that they hadn't seen anyone by or around his cubicle all day.

Shawn returned to his desk, a little irritated and beside himself. What the hell was this all about?

He finally had the gumption to approach the urn again, gingerly setting himself down in his swiveling chair and pulling the seat up to the edge of the desk, the urn now sitting right before him. It was stout, no more than a foot high, with a bulbous shape to its top that slimmed down gradually as it reached the base of its golden self. Shawn wondered what was in the urn; he hoped it would be anything other than what was *always* in an urn. But the note made it clear what he'd find when he opened the lid.

Nevertheless, the mystery of the strange thing got the better of him. He reached out, grabbing hold of the urn with both hands, consciously commanding them not to tremble. He lifted the container and set it on his lap, the metal chilled against his warm, living skin. He grabbed hold of the round knob of the lid and pulled it off. He peeked into the urn, letting the fluorescent lighting in the call-center shine over what lay within.

Dark gray ash filled the golden urn to the brim.

That chill weaseled its way across the back of his neck again. He had no doubt what the ashes had once been, prior to their current dusty state.

They had been a person—living and breathing and thinking, just as Shawn was. But now that person was dead. Dead and cremated to ash. And in his hands.

Shawn put the lid back on and set the urn on his desk, unconsciously rubbing his hands against the fabric of his pants. He swallowed loud and hard, breathing out through his nose in a stressed rush. He rubbed his forehead, massaging his temples to relieve the onset of pressure that was now there.

Were the ashes those of Carl Blanch, whoever the hell he was?

This was just too weird for him. But he had to find

out what was going on. And he knew that if he wanted to find some semblance of understanding, he would have to find out who this Carl Blanch was, first.

"*Psst*! Shawn!"

It was Clay, leaning up and over his cubicle and looking at Shawn, whispering urgently. He was pointing off to something on the other side of Shawn's cube. "Matthews is coming, man! Get back to work or she'll chew your ass out!"

Shawn broke out of his quizzical thoughts. He grabbed hold of the urn, wondering where he could stash it. He didn't want anyone walking by, seeing it, and questioning things that he himself had no answers to. He opened up an empty drawer of his, setting the urn in there with a careful ease. He grabbed the slip of paper that'd come with it and set it in there, as well, and then shut the drawer.

He turned his computer back on and got to work, continuing to toil away until his workday was over. He didn't spare another glance at the urn or the note, but his inquiries into their nature were never far from his mind, no matter what work he had to do or what calls he had to answer.

He felt the urge to pull the urn back out now and again. To set it on his desk and simply stare at it. To open it up and look at the ashes, and to wonder what fire had created them, what blaze had molded them into what they now were.

Fire . . .

But he kept at his work, answering phone calls dutifully until it was time to go home.

***

Shawn would do a web search for Carl Blanch—type in his name on a search engine and see if anything stood out or could be of use to him. Maybe he'd find some article or profile on the man, find out if he lived in the immediate area or not. Maybe he'd even find an obituary dedicated to the mystery-man, if it were indeed his ashes in the urn.

Shawn had been tempted to do the search on his office computer. He'd finished his workday at 5 o'clock, and could easily do his perusing of the web at his desk. But he opted out, deciding to grab the urn from its spot in his drawer and take it home with him. He was tired, and he'd feel more comfortable doing his task in the comfort of his own home—if there was any comfort at all when it came to searching for possible dead men. Covering the urn up with his jacket, he left work, smiling and nodding at those he passed, not betraying that anything was out of the usual.

He'd sped home as quickly as he could, passing down each street and road several miles per hour over the limit. The urn was sitting in the passenger seat next to him. He'd set it upright, settling the seatbelt over it to keep it in place, just as if it were a living person.

Halfway home, he was forced to come to a halt. Fire engines, police cars, and a few other vehicles stuck in the hectic rush of coming home from work were stopped along Wilson Street, an apparent emergency in progress.

Whatever was going on, Shawn saw that the fire trucks and police cars were situated a few houses up ahead. People were getting out of their cars all around him, walking up to see what was going on.

Cursing, and with nothing better to do, Shawn stepped out of his car and joined the flock of people taking in the spectacle ahead.

Some house was burning down, its three stories already engulfed in fire.

Shawn stared at the blazing household, unblinking. As others around him chatted in whispers, speculating as to what caused the fire and if anyone was hurt because of it, he simply stared, silent and watching in awe.

The fire was utterly raging. Red and orange flames slithered out of window frames whose glass had exploded outwards from the pressure and the heat. The front door of the household was a conflagration, the flames spilling out and stretching up to the sky, like demons' tongues licking at the heavens that forsook them. The walls of the house were crumbling away, falling in charred clumps as the flames ate away at the home's insides. The shingled roof of the house was creaking audibly over the rushing breath of the blaze; it would no doubt tumble and fall in a matter of moments, another casualty to the fire.

Police were trying to guide the growing crowd away from the house, asking the onlookers to give more room for the firefighters to operate. Not that it mattered, really. The dozen men garbed in their yellow and black suits held and aimed their water hoses in futility; the water, like the house, was simply being consumed, and gratefully so, by the growing blaze.

The fire would not be stopped, until it'd had its fill of the house and anything else it wished to burn away. It would only stop when it *chose* to do so.

In that moment, standing among the mumbling crowd of onlookers, Shawn was struck by the sheer power and ferocity that was fire.

Even though they were two full households away from the burning house, he could feel the heat of the fire warming his face. To think that something could hold such force and energy as to be felt from so far off. It made him feel humble, that power. He'd never really stopped to consider the sheer force that fire was, that it had; it could create and mold, destroy or raze—whatever its disposition was at the time it sparked into its awesome life. No matter how humanity sought to control and use it for its own needs, they could never truly contain it; it would eventually break free and scold them, if it was of the mind to do so. To say man had invented it was a shame to its nature; fire *willed* itself to be.

It chose what it wished to incinerate; and it often chose to burn everything.

Shawn wondered what it would be like to step into that fire; to be consumed by it, absorbed and remolded by its whim; to be a part of that awesome power he had never before understood or felt; to know true power before he became ash . . .

The voice of a police officer shook him out of his thoughts, pressing a firm hand against his chest and forcing Shawn backwards.

"What the hell are you doing, pal?" the officer asked.

Shawn looked at him, confused. He hadn't realized that he had walked clear past the other speculators and was moving towards the burning house, almost beside the first phalanx of fire fighters.

"Get back, sir. Get back!"

Shawn nodded his complacency to the officer and stepped away, not taking his eyes off the fire. It burned on, the home it had started in now a hollow husk and on its last limbs of existence. Shawn finally turned back around, walking through the still-chattering crowd and going back to his car. He opened the door and set himself in his seat, grasping the steering wheel with a hard clutch.

He turned to the urn. His curious reflection looked back at him.

He jumped when a horn blared behind him. He glanced around, noticing that the police were signaling the cars on the street to drive on, and the car behind him was ready to get on their way.

Shawn put his car in gear and drove on slowly, keeping the pace of the vehicles before him. He turned on the radio to try and keep his mind off of things, off of fire and ash.

As he drove by the unfortunate house—which was now just a charred foundation of black smoke and gray remains—he didn't spare it another glance.

He wanted to look. But he didn't.

***

Shawn arrived home without further incident. He parked his car in the garage, grabbed the urn, and went into his house, determined to try and solve the mystery of the container, its note, and why he had received them.

He was now sitting at his computer in the living room. The urn was on his desk, a foot away from his elbow, like a faithful friend looking on with him as he prepared to search the web.

Google was up on the screen, the cursor over the search box and ready for something to be typed into it. The only thing was, Shawn didn't know exactly what to search for.

He knew he was looking for anything relating to a Carl Blanch, and preferably one that lived in town or the immediate community.

It was as good of a start as any, so he typed in the man's name and the name of the town. He hit the enter key, hoping with all his will that something useful would come up instantaneously. After a quick second of loading, a page of related sites and articles popped up on the screen. He looked to the first entry on the list.

It looked like an article from the local newspaper. "MAN COMMITS SUICIDE BY SELF-IMMOLATION," the link read.

The article was dated from a week ago. An image of

a smiling middle-aged man was set next to the bold print of the title. He wore a green and black flannel shirt and was completely bald, his wrinkling skin showing his age. Thin, rectangular glasses sat on a beaked nose and over gray-blue eyes. He looked happy.

Beneath the picture were two words: "Carl Blanch."

Shawn looked away from the screen and over to the urn.

"Hello, Carl," he said politely. "Nice to meet you."

He turned back to his computer and clicked on the link to the article. The website for the local newspaper came up, and the article was there before him. He started reading slowly, taking in every detail:

```
 Police and forensic investigators are baffled
by the recent apparent suicide of 68 year-old
Carl Blanch, a retired factory-worker and Marsden
resident who seems to have taken his own life by
setting himself on fire.
 Police arrived at Blanch's household on the
afternoon of Wednesday, July 30th in response to
an emergency call. Police Chief Andrew Mahaney,
one of several officers on the scene, described
their arrival at Blanch's residence. "When we
walked into the home, the air was thick with the
smell of smoke. My men and I were choking, it was
```

so strong. When we entered the living room, we found Mr. Blanch's ashes scattered on the floor, a box of matches spilled out over the carpet, and an emptied gas-can not far off."

Maria Blanch, Carl Blanch's elder sister and fellow Marsden resident, was the one to make the emergency call to authorities. Maria Blanch claims she went to her brother's home after having attempted to call him multiple times in recent days, calls which went unanswered and without further response from her sibling.

Maria Blanch states that she was in constant contact with her brother and that the two spoke over the phone each day, and that his unanswered calls were highly uncharacteristic of him. She maintains that he showed no signs of depression or other tell-tale suicidal tendencies prior to his death.

The unusual mode of suicide forced investigators to question whether or not Blanch's death was by his own hand and not a result of foul-play. However, no items or valuables belonging to Blanch were revealed to be missing, nor were there any evident signs of struggle or conflict from a possible perpetrator. Police found a note confirmed to be written in Blanch's hand, relating his intentions to commit self-immolation. Police Chief Mahaney stated the note was "dubious" but would not elaborate further regarding its subject matter.

Investigators are further puzzled by the

nature of the fire that claimed Blanch's life. Keith Welt, arson expert for the Marsden police, stated that the fire and its effects on the surrounding area of the living room were "unlike anything [he'd] seen before."

"The carpet and ceiling of the room were neither singed nor burnt, nor were any items of furniture," Welt claims. "Almost all fires will show signs of charring or burning on surrounding items and areas, especially where gasoline is concerned. These signs, however, aren't to be found in this instance, where the deceased set the fire."

Welt says it appeared as if the fire burnt only Blanch's body, and if it weren't for the heavy smell of smoke and the remains found there, he wouldn't have assumed there'd been a fire set in the house at any point.

Further insight into Blanch's motives in his suicide is being sought out by police. Any information regarding this matter is welcomed by authorities.

The deceased's funeral arrangements have yet to be released.

Shawn finished the article and leaned back in his chair, sighing out his frustrations.

So, the mysterious Carl Blanch had killed himself.

And he'd done it by setting himself on fire, of all ways to go about it. "Why" was far from anyone's understanding, apparently—especially to Shawn. He still had no clue who the man was. No memories of chance encounters with the guy or the casual mentioning of his name in friendly conversation leapt to mind.

Shawn simply didn't know the man. So why was he given his ashes?

That was what drove Shawn's mind into a frenzy. Suicide was understandable, to a degree; what didn't make any sense was why someone would give another's ashes to a complete and total stranger. Why had Blanch's ashes been scooped up off the floor of his living room only to be tossed in an urn and left on Shawn's desk?

The "dubious" note. That was something that stuck out to Shawn as he read the article. Maybe that note had some confounding requests regarding *him* in some strange way; maybe that was why he now had Carl Blanch's ashes sitting right beside him.

Ashes to ashes, me to you.

Perhaps that mystery note had been written just before or after Blanch wrote his own suicide note, declaring his intentions of death by fire. But still, why Shawn? That was the burning question—pun unintended.

Shawn rubbed a hand over the urn, patting its cool,

golden side like the shoulder of a friend.

"Carl, buddy," he whispered, "I don't know who you were or why you did what you did, but you had issues, pal. Serious fucking issues."

His mind turned back to the fire he had seen at the burning house just an hour ago. Twisting flames. Staggering heat. Ineffable power. Those were the exact same things Carl Blanch had last known in this world.

Again, Shawn wondered what it would be like to step into fire, how it would feel to have a pyre held in the simple skin of your hand. Would it be agony or glory, to feel such a thing?

A yawn came to him, and he stretched his arms and arched his back, feeling the work and worry of the day taking its toll on him all of a sudden. He felt tired, and sleep sounded wonderful to him now that part of his curiosity towards the day's strange events had been sated. He stood up from his desk, shutting down the computer and grabbing the urn.

He made his way across the room, over to the mantle of his small fireplace. He scooted a picture of his mother, father, and sister on the middle of the mantle aside, making room. He set the urn in the free spot. Shawn may not have known Carl Blanch, but the guy had been a person just like himself, and his remains were deserving of some respect; this spot seemed respectful enough, at least for now.

Shawn gave the urn another pat. "Good night, Carl."

He turned around, leaving the living room and making his way up the stairs. He went into his bedroom, his bed and their sheets a welcome sight to his weary self. He fell down onto the sheets, not bothering to kick off his shoes or change his clothes.

He was asleep in moments.

***

The dream was glorious.

The forest he stood in had once been large and filled with trees of all heights, all species, and all ages. But that forest was no more. It had been remade, replaced. Made new, made better.

The ground was covered in a thick layer of ash, every hue and tone of gray from dark to light found somewhere within the ankle-deep covering. A slight breeze moved along the smoky air, sending the ash scurrying in thin drifts all along the expansive vista that had been formed from the forest's razing. Charred, black stumps that'd once been trees popped up here and there, breaking the gray, dusty surface. Off in the distance, a city of skyscrapers and towers rose into the gray sky. Their metal frames and glass exteriors were all aflame with swaying fires, candles to light this new and better world he had been shown.

Now, all that remained was for Shawn to become a part of it all.

Carl Blanch stood before him, among the layer of ash. He looked as he had in the picture of the article that had detailed his death.

No; not his death. His transformation.

The only difference in the man was that the eyes behind his thin-rimmed glasses were pure flame, shifting and wavering in his sockets—alive. The fire had become his innards, his spirit, his *true* essence, and it shone through eyes that were once human, but which were now something far greater.

Blanch extended his right arm. A ball of red, orange, and yellow fire rolled and shifted in the palm of his bare hand. Both men looked at it with awe and appreciation.

"Ashes to ashes, me to you," Blanch whispered in reverence, and he handed the blazing ball to Shawn.

Shawn accepted it into his own grasp. It was a burning blessing to him as he felt its heat and held its form.

Around him, the ashes on the ground were rising up to the sky, forming sheets of tumbling, pure gray, like the walls of a brewing tornado. Blanch's skin and clothes turned gray, and he began to break apart in flakes of ash that joined the growing tumult rising in the air. The fire in Shawn's hand broke its form, slithering over his body in tendrils, covering his arm, then his chest, then his legs, and finally his face, spreading and covering his whole body in an epidermis of flame.

It felt like grace.

With burning eyes that cried joyful tears of sparks, he stared up to the sky. The torrents of ash swirled around and above him. Then, all at once, the ash descended down on him, washing over his flame-riddled body and taking him, making him a part of their world.

And he was glad.

***

Shawn looked around at the call-center, taking in the people and the things in his cubicle. They all seemed somehow . . . superfluous to him.

Staring at computer screens, chatting about random and senseless things with one another on meager breaks, answering phone calls from people that were never satisfied with he and his coworkers' efforts in aiding them. Small, confining cubicles that held you in far better than the bars of a prison, chained not by cuffs but by the mundane and the staggering average. The only reason he had even come to work this morning was out of pure habit and a now failing sense of duty.

It all made him feel powerless.

His dream a week ago had awoken something in him—a greater understanding of the world, both as it was and as he hoped it could be. But the latter was nowhere in sight now, not in the everyday dealings of his life and their lack-luster purposes. He longed for something more.

Perhaps Carl Blanch had felt the same way. Perhaps he knew the way to find that something-more, that something-better.

Shawn looked over his cubicle and around the call-center again. No one was paying any attention to him or his scrutinizations. He took that as a sign, as a chance. He grabbed his jacket, turned off his computer, disconnected the phone on his desk, and left his cubicle.

No one paid him any mind as he simply walked out of the office.

***

Shawn stopped off at a dollar store before returning home.

He picked up some oddball things: a few packs of gum, a paperback novel he had no intention of reading, some cooking utensils that wouldn't make it out of their container, and a plastic gas can. The gas can was the only thing he really wanted, but he felt like the other items shielded him somehow, masked any intentions that his face and the look in his eyes might betray. He didn't want anyone to see his intention and talk him out of it, not when the truth of things had finally been revealed to him.

But the girl at the checkout didn't notice anything odd. She simply smiled, accepted his money, bagged the items, and let him go on his way.

He drove to a Shell station afterwards and put ten dollars' worth of gas into his new gas can. Then he was homeward bound.

He parked his car in his garage and went inside, gas can in hand and mind set on doing what he felt had to be done. He liked the sound gasoline made, sloshing against the plastic of the can.

He set the can down in the living room and threw the bag of his other dollar-store buys in the trash. He went into the kitchen and opened a drawer by the sink. An old box of matches was right at the top of all the clutter in the drawer. Convenient. He snatched the box, the little wooden sticks inside rattling as he stepped over to his landline phone, grabbing the Yellow Pages sitting beside it. With the box and the phone book in hand, he went back into the living room.

He sat down at his computer desk, setting the box of matches off to the side and opening up the phone book. He thumbed through it randomly, not looking for any specific number or name, shuffling through the pages like a deck of cards before a fateful game. He finally stopped at a random page, setting the phone book down. He closed his eyes, hovered his finger over the page, revolving his hand around and around in a circular motion. He brought his index finger down on a whim. He opened his eyes and looked at what name his finger rested on.

Janice Sanford.

Shawn wondered if this was the way he had been chosen. He'd like to think it was. Randomly receiving the knowledge he had been given was an exhilarating thought; it made the process seem magical—Russian Roulette for the lucky. Bestowing his understanding—his gift—in the same fashion seemed only fitting.

He set the phone book aside and reached for a pen and two pages of printer paper. He wrote his wishes and reasoning for what was to follow on the first, stating what he wanted done with his remains once they had been discovered. He wondered if his own sister would be the one to find him; it could happen.

On the second piece of paper, he wrote his other, much briefer message—the one that actually mattered and held the most importance. He left both pieces of paper on the desk, certain whoever found him would come across them, hoping they would fulfill his requests.

Shawn grabbed the box of matches with a steady hand and walked over to the gas can. As he walked by the mantle, he looked over Carl Blanch's urn.

"See you soon, Carl."

He set the matches down on the floor and hoisted up the gas can. He popped the top off, the odor of the fumes wafting through the air instantly. He held his head back and poured the gas over himself, letting it soak his skin and his clothes, making sure he was covered in the liquid. He tossed the empty can off to the side, its hollow self banging along the floor.

He knelt down and grabbed the matches. He slid the covering back and picked out a single stick. He stared expectantly at the small red head of the match. He could feel the power brewing in and around him, waiting to be unleashed.

Shawn stood up, setting the match-head against the strip of the box. He sighed, embracing that exaltation of his coming transformation. He scraped the match against the box in a quick blur of motion and threw the box away.

The flames took him immediately. And just like in his dream, he wept.

***

The urn was just sitting on her porch step when she came out to grab the paper.

Janice Sanford wondered who had left it and why she had been the one to receive it. The note left in front of the urn made no sense to her and explained nothing:

"Ashes to ashes, me to you — Shawn Dwyer"

Carly's Seventh

"I hope that isn't what I think it is," Amanda grumbled, looking out into the dining room and over at Paul's mystery present.

She turned back to her husband with a probing glance, slowly handing him the last of the bowls. Paul just gave her a quick shrug, avoiding eye contact and scooting away from her as he set the bowls out for the cake and ice cream that would come later on.

That just made Amanda even more suspicious of him.

Her husband had snuck the present out and set it among Carly's other gifts while she'd finished up the decorating. It dwarfed their daughter's other presents by comparison, taking up a good deal of space at the end of the table and looking like a mountain behind the stacks of dolls, books, and play make-up kits they'd gotten her. Paul had given the mystery gift a cute kitty-cat wrap-job, deviating from Amanda's idea of a Peppa Pig theme. Peppa tablecloth, Peppa plates, Peppa balloons, Peppa cake, Peppa wrapping paper—and a now this giant box clad with kittens, impossible to miss and guaranteed to catch Carly's eye.

That he'd decided to just spring this on her without any warning was one thing; but if the present turned out to be what Amanda expected, that was a whole other matter.

Paul had been adamant in getting Carly something special—something very specific, big, and expensive—for quite a while now. Something that he'd sworn up and down she would love. Amanda, though, had been far less assured of his idea. She'd caught the glint in her husband's eye every time he'd offhandedly mentioned it, had seen the extra pep in his step every time they conveniently walked past one at Wal-Mart. It hadn't taken much for her to realize that Paul wanted it for Carly more than Carly could ever want it for herself.

It was one of those cases where a parent thought they were going all out for their child, when in reality, they were indulging in their own peculiar hang-up, forcing their interest onto the child. Amanda had experienced it herself when she was Carly's age. My Little Pony had just become the big thing back then, and her mother had simply fallen for the fad. For the whole next year, her mother had bought her nearly every bit of pony merchandise she could find—despite the fact that Amanda hardly ever bothered to play with them. Her mother had liked it, so she'd wanted Amanda to like it, too. That's all there was to it, and now Paul had been doing the same deal. And he may have just bought the proverbial pony.

"I'm serious, Paul," Amanda said, rummaging through a kitchen drawer for a utility lighter. She kept her voice as low as she could, just in case Carly came rushing in and overheard them. "If you went and got that stupid thing behind my back, you and I are going to have a serious talk later."

Paul gave another maddening shrug as he walked to the freezer and grabbed the tub of chocolate ice cream from inside. "Even *if* I did get it, I don't see why it'd bother you so much."

He spoke in such a nonplussed, matter of fact way that it sent a bit of heat underneath Amanda's skin. He brushed past her and set the ice cream on the table. "And why is it 'stupid' all of a sudden, huh?"

"Well, it's expensive, especially for all we already spent on Carly this year; it's bulky, and we'll have to find somewhere to keep it; and you won't admit to yourself that maybe she won't like it as much as you hope she will."

Paul scoffed through his nose and set his hands to his hips. He tried to keep some playfulness in his voice, but Amanda could clearly hear the condescension beneath it.

"Oh, come on! It didn't cost that much and it won't be at all hard to store! And I do think she'll like it—and I also think that *you don't* like it, so you don't want her to have it!"

"And *I think* you're just trying to force it on her before she's even ready!"

Paul scoffed again. "Oh, really? Well, what about—?"

"Is everything ready?" Carly called out from the living room. They heard the sound of their daughter rushing down the hall, closing in on the dining room with an excitement that could no longer be contained.

Carly came skidding around the corner, immediately gawking at her presents and her mother's decorations. Amanda saw her daughter's eyes widen all the more when they caught sight of Paul's gigantic present.

Carly gave a squeal, jumping up and down. "Can I go ahead and make my wish first and then open my presents?"

Amanda gave a sigh, sending a quick *This isn't over*-look towards Paul. She turned right back to Carly, speaking cheerily. "Sure, honey. Let's light 'em up!"

The family stepped over to the table, Carly hopping up into a chair, Paul dimming the lights for effect, and Amanda striking up the utility lighter. She watched its little tongue of flame flick about for a moment with a smile on her face, then set to lighting all fifty-three candles around the pink-icing face of Peppa Pig. It had been her idea to surround the design with as many candles as she could fit on there, placing them so tightly together that it made a veritable wall of wax around the cartoon character's round head.

Amanda lit them slowly, savoring the sight of each wick as it caught fire and going gradually around, until a circle of flame had formed. She could feel their heat upon the skin of her hand, warming it with such a thrilling sensation. She found it to be so beautiful . . .

Paul cleared his throat pointedly. Amanda gave him a side glance, seeing the incredulous look on his face in the flickering light of the candles. *Come on, already*, he said without speaking a word.

Amanda flicked the lighter off and leaned back. She started singing "Happy Birthday," Paul picking up the tune with her as Carly arched over the cake, prepped and anxious to make her wish. She let out a huge puff of breath, snuffing the candles after a couple extra puffs. Her parents gave her a round of applause.

"Can I open my presents now?" Carly asked without missing a beat.

Amanda said she could, and the seven year old was tearing into the first of them before Paul could flick the lights back on.

Carly tore through her gifts with zeal, squealing with each unveiling and thanking her parents up and down. She whittled away at the pile of presents—until only Paul's mystery gift remained. As Carly set her hands to it, Amanda glanced her husband's way. His eyes were wide and his lips were turned up in mischievous anticipation, and he was leaning in to watch their daughter open it.

Carly ripped away at the paper, a big flap of it tearing away from the side and revealing the box beneath. Amanda couldn't help but groan when she saw the Ryobi brand name on the box's top corner, with the words "14 in. 40-Volt Lithium-Ion Brushless Cordless Chainsaw" scrawled under it.

"*So cool*!" Carly fawned, doing a little dance in her chair as she unwrapped the rest of it. She beamed at the image of the lime-green saw on the box's broad side.

Amanda reached out, grabbed Paul's elbow, and pulled him over to her. She started scolding him as quietly as she could manage, though their daughter was still fully intent on the surprise gift.

"Damn it, Paul! I told you we shouldn't get that yet!"

Paul kept up the covert argument. "That's what you *said*, but what you meant was that we shouldn't get it at all! Right? Come on, look at her! She loves it!"

"I just don't think she's ready for that yet! It's not safe. You're forcing it on her. Besides, maybe she doesn't want to do it your way!"

Paul scoffed and gave her a knowing look. "Oh, really? *I'm* forcing it on her? Well, what about the new gas-can you got for her last week and told her to keep secret from me?"

Amanda went into stunned and embarrassed silence for a moment. She'd been caught, she knew it, and she had no real rebuttal.

"Well, I'm just . . . trying to show her that there are other ways to . . ."

"Oh, sure! Other ways, meaning *your* way! And how is using a chainsaw to do it any less safe than setting them *on fire*? Hell, she could burn the house down before she even gets to kill her first one!"

While the couple was busy debating, Carly had left the table to get a drink from the kitchen. As she came back into the dining room, something outside the window caught her attention. She looked out at the front yard, smiling big, and then shouted in excitement.

"Uncle George is here! Uncle George is here!"

Amanda and Paul turned to see their daughter running out of the room and towards the front door. They quickly looked back at each other, both with worried looks on their faces.

"Oh, jeez . . ." Amanda groaned, looking towards the chainsaw. "If he sees that . . ."

"Go get Carly and I'll hide it!" Paul stammered.

The couple bolted off, Paul lugging the gift away and into another room as Amanda rushed down the hall. Carly had left the door wide open and her mother went running through it and out into the evening.

Her daughter had been right. Paul's older brother had just shown up, the exhaust from his old Ford Contour still wafting out from behind it. George had already gotten out of the car and was standing by the sidewalk as Carly came running up to him, giving him a big hug.

"Happy birthday, munchkin!" he told her, laughing as she hopped around him.

"Uncle George, guess what! Mommy and daddy got me a chainsaw for my birthday!"

Shit, Amanda thought in dismay. She ran up to them and set her hands to Carly's shoulder, greeting George with a strained smile. *Shit!*

George just looked at her funny, neither saying a thing to each other. Amanda heard Paul dashing up beside her and decided to let him handle it. He'd bought the damn thing, after all.

"Hey, George!" Paul said happily, setting his arm around Amanda to set the pretense. "How've . . . ?"

"You got your little girl a chainsaw?" George interrupted, obviously dumbfounded. "Not a real chainsaw, right?"

Dismayed that the act was already crumbling, Paul hesitated. "Well, uhm . . . I mean . . ."

Uncle George looked beside himself with shock. "God, you did. *That's* what you got her? What in the hell's wrong with you, Paul?"

Paul shook his head and made to defend himself, but George cut him off again.

"A chainsaw . . . that's just not satisfying enough. If you really want to get some thrills out of a kill, an axe is the way to go! Put your back and your frustrations into it!"

Amanda and Paul looked at each other, trying not to roll their eyes. They knew that George would give them crap over the chainsaw, as he always did when the topic of their individual methods came up. They'd wanted to avoid the criticism and the hailing of his almighty axe, but that was out the window now.

Uncle George gave the parents a sad and judging shake of his head. But then he smiled down at his niece.

"After all, we have the princess of power here! She could lift and bring that axe down like no one's business, right sweetheart?"

Carly giggled and gave her uncle another big hug as he looked back to Amanda and Paul.

"Besides, you don't just give a kid a chainsaw! That's like giving them a bat and no baseball! She has to have something to *use* it on!"

George put on a mischievous smile and reached for the backseat door. He let it swing open with a hearty "ta-da!"

A teenage boy lay across the backseat, his whole body wrapped in floral paper and bound in rope. Muffled pleas came from his gagged mouth as he looked out at the family, tears in his eyes. George had put a huge, neat red bow across the teenager's forehead.

"Luckily, the fun uncle has got you covered, sweetie!" George said, patting Carly's shoulder. "I picked it up at a Toys R' Us just last week!"

Carly did another excited dance and squeezed her uncle's leg. "Thank you *so* much, Uncle George! This is so, *so* cool!"

George gave Amanda and Paul a shit-eating grin and a knowing nod. The couple just looked to each other again and shrugged, each figuring that their little girl's birthday was as monumental a time as any for her to get her first kill.

"Can we go ahead and do it, Mom and Dad?" Carly wheeled around and begged them.

Before either could answer, Uncle George was saying: "Well, of course you can! What good's a party without a piñata, of sorts? I'll even let you borrow my axe, kiddo! Got it in the trunk. Or you can use that loud and bulky new chainsaw, I suppose . . ."

"And don't forget the gas-can mommy got you," Amanda couldn't help but put in excitedly. Paul gave her a *Really?*-look, but she shrugged it off.

"Well, what's it going to be, sweetie?" Paul asked. "What do you want to use on Uncle George's gift?"

Carly had a serious, pondering look on her face as she thought it over. She glanced back at the still-struggling teenager, who was rolling about and trying to scream out for help.

Then, Carly smiled big.

"Can't I try a bit of all three?"

Amanda, Paul, and Uncle George looked at each other, smiling a little bitterly.

"Sure, honey," Amanda finally answered. "It's your birthday, after all. We'll have cake and ice cream afterwards."

Goodnight's Alternative Carnival of Curiosities

"Sold!" the auctioneer called out with a rap from her little gavel. The hall—which had been filled to standing room three hours before, but which was now nearly emptied—echoed with the hard smack. Two of the auction house's suited associates moved to wheel away the latest item from the block, a vintage framed poster for *The Cabinet of Dr. Caligari*, sold for $7,500; as they left, so did the item's buyer, leaving only a dozen or so spectators sitting in a sea of folding chairs.

Most lounged in their seats, slumped and slack from the last hours and the bidding battles that had come with them. Though they remained in attendance, it was more to simply see and admire the last of the day's items than having an intention to purchase them; their bidding paddles rested on their knees as they stifled yawns and blinked tiredly. Only one of them remained straight and alert, paddle at the ready in one a hand, an ornate, black cane clasped in the other. His long, scruffy locks were bundled and bound in a tie and tracing down his back. A piqued glint had sparked in his dark eyes throughout the entirety of the auction. It matched the sheen of his dark suit.

He shuffled in his seat a tad as the auctioneer looked back out to the crowd from her box. She spoke into the microphone, her voice reverberating like the voice of God.

"We're nearing the end of today's proceedings, my friends." She cleared her throat nervously before continuing on. "The reputation of our next item precedes itself."

Behind her, on a large white screen, images of the item began to shuffle by. They were of a great, black contraption, taken from all manner of sides and angles to capture the thing's enormity and detail, a thing far too large to wheel out onto the stage and display for the spectators. The man with the dark eyes and dark suit leaned forward in his chair, gawking at the photos, a mischievous grin twisting his bearded face.

"The Vernaldi Organ comes to us courtesy of Donald Matheson, the current consignor of the lot. The item is regarded to be in fine condition and working order, with all operations and capabilities intact. Minor upkeep and necessary alterations have been previously made to maintain the mechanics. Included are documents certifying the item's authenticity. It has been appraised at $10,000; this is also its reserve price, so we shall start the bidding at this amount. Do I have $10,000?"

The dark-suited man's arm shot up, paddle in hand. The auctioneer nodded his way, seeming a tad taken aback by his brash enthusiasm.

"I have $10,000. Do I have eleven?"

The hall and its occupiers went utterly silent. No one made a show of consideration, much less a move to outbid the dark-suited man. The stillness, though, was not out of sheer indifference to the item, for each and every eye was fixated on the screen and the images of the huge black organ slowly shifting by; it seemed instead a stillness born of humbled uncertainty.

"Do I have $11,000?" the auctioneer asked again. She received no response from the crowd. She opted to get on with it.

"$10,000 going once. Twice. Sold, for $10,000." She gave another sharp crack of her gavel and moved to scribble a note down on whatever lay before her. "The winning bidder may claim the item from the house's warehouse following the close of the proceedings."

But the dark-suited man wasn't there to hear it. He'd risen from his seat and hurriedly left the hall the moment he had won his much sought-after prize.

***

Silas Goodnight (who'd legally changed his name from Matthew Crumb, shortly after becoming the owner of his Alternative Carnival of Curiosities) walked past the auction house's guard and into the establishment's warehouse, having been given the okay to enter and claim his grand purchase. He gave his cane a playful twirl as he followed the guard's directions, wandering among the house's many other lots and rarities to where the organ rested. He wandered through the shelves and flanks of antiques taking up the musty space of the place as though he were Dorothy on the road to Oz—an overjoyed jaunt towards a much-desired goal.

His carnival had catered to a particular clientele ever since its creation three years ago, the "alternative" in its title referring to the more adult crowds who appreciated the bizarre, the strange, and the downright demented. Kiddy slides, flying elephant rides, and the like weren't to be found at his venues. No, sir; not at all. If it wasn't odd or peculiar in a rather *Twilight Zone* sort of fashion, it had no place at the Carnival of Curiosities. And Silas, who'd taken a simple passion for the dark and twisted and turned it into a lucrative business, was always on the lookout for the next weird act or eye-catching exhibit.

One item, in particular, had come across his eccentric radar long before the Carnival of Curiosities had even been established. He'd first heard of it by sticking his ear into various carnie circles, its reputation spoken of in either grand jest or nervous whispers. The stories circling the organ had enthralled him from the get-go, and he'd soon begun his search for the infamous item, wondering if it even existed, or if it was just some urban legend of the entertainment world.

It existed, alright, and after all his research, and after all this time, he had it. It was his. And as he took one last left turn, it was right there before him, sitting aside from all the other items in its lonesomeness, its grandness, and its menace.

He now realized that the dark magnificence of the organ could only be truly appreciated in person; the photos shown in the auction, along with those he'd turned up on the internet, did it no justice at all.

The early twentieth century fairground organ was roughly 6 x 18 x 10 feet, by Silas' eye; quite colossal, even by the typical standards for this style of organ. Its wooden bulk had been predominately painted black, save for its sculptures and some silver trimming and filigree for character. Its sides and its back held a reflective glimmer—like oil—as light poured down onto it from the warehouse's high windows; the front piece of the contraption remained shrouded in shadow, looking all the darker in its hue. It was this darkened face of the machine that begged the eye's attention, and Silas took in its design as a devotee would an age-old cathedral.

The organ seemed split into three halves, each with its own contribution to the grander vision of the thing. Its lowest portion had been carved to mimic column-work, with four ridged shafts in total (two on each edge, another two closer to the center), leaving depressed bits of panel in between—the sunken cheeks to its gaunt face. On the outer side of the central columns hung the dark gray figures of two immaculately crafted sculptures, mirroring each other with an artisan's flair. They looked like gargoyles, their muscled bodies hugging the columns, their claws digging into them to hang there with bat wings about their shoulders, fanged mouths drawn wide and tails snaking around the column down to their hooked feet. Between the central columns and the creatures was a circular web-work of interlacing and overlapping lines, not unlike some mystic Celtic knot; if they had any meaning beyond their simple lavishness, Silas did not know what it could be.

The upper third of the organ was an arch, with rounded nubs and curved designs made to look like clouds stretching along the top. Set within the clouds were the cream colored faces of woeful looking babes gazing downwards; perhaps cherubs crying in a troubled heaven.

The middle section was largely hollowed out into a cabinet, displaying the layered rows of bronze pipes arranged within. They would shake off their gathered dust soon enough. They would play the thing's storied music once more. Silas ached to hear it for himself.

Situated in the center of the cabinet was perhaps the most curious quality of the organ: a three and a half foot figure of a light gray, nude man, finely sculpted and with arms hanging out to his sides, palms out in a show of impunity. Or perhaps even welcome. His head was peculiarly hairless and completely featureless—just a smooth, blank oval set upon his neck. The effect was both unnerving and unnatural.

As Silas moved in closer to appreciate this odd character, he heard someone stepping up beside him. He was surprised to see the organ's former owner, famed electronics mogul Donald Matheson, staring at the organ along with him.

"Mr. Matheson," Silas said with an appreciative nod. "You have my thanks for finally putting this rarity up for sale, along with the thanks of the rest of my little carnival. It's sure to fit right in with our troupe."

Matheson gave him a slow once-over before looking back to the organ. "My pleasure, I assure you. I've, uh, heard a small deal about your 'alternative' carnival; I've yet to attend, myself. As for the organ, I'd nearly thought there wouldn't be any interest in a . . . well-traveled item such as this."

Silas smiled at the millionaire's modest evasion of the organ's past. "Yes; its history—for those who know of it—would no doubt scare off most. But that is *precisely* why I have longed to own it as long as I have. I'd nearly sought you out once before, when I'd heard you acquired it."

Matheson turned a wary eye back to him. "So, you've done your homework, eh?"

Silas began to circle the organ. As he proudly strode about, he lapsed into recounting all that his research and efforts had unearthed about the organ's history. He relished the telling, seeing it as practice, for when he would tell it to his carnival's visitors this season.

"The Vernaldi Organ—named so after its creator, Piero Vernaldi. Dubbed "an Einstein of the arts" in later years; a prodigy as an artist in both sculpture and paint, and a versed musician in a number of instruments and styles. A true virtuoso. He'd achieved national fame before he'd even struck thirty, performing various concerts and filling galleries by the time of 1928, entertaining all who had the mind, the time, and the money for it. But then the galas and showings stopped one day; Vernaldi shut himself away in his home, all to work on something new. Something grand. This very organ.

"For the next year, he toiled away at creating the machine, becoming a noted recluse and taking few visitors—even family. Few ever saw the organ, at least, not until its completion. The one notable exception was Vernaldi's brother, Luca, who stopped by unannounced one day. He was chased out by Piero, and he later wrote in his personal journal of how frightened he was by his brother's appearance and attitude, as well as the "haunting hulk that was his work.""

"You have, indeed, done your homework," Matheson cut in with a disconcerted mumble. Silas ignored it and kept on with the tale.

"Luca died within that very week. Trampled by a carriage. Even his demise could not tear Vernaldi from his work; he did not attend his brother's funeral and kept stolidly to the organ, until August of 1929, when he had finally finished his masterpiece. Vernaldi celebrated the achievement by taking a pistol and shooting himself in the mouth, to the astonishment of all who knew him.

"His family quickly sold the organ to a carnival just outside of Verona, wanting nothing to do with the thing that had stolen their relative from them. One month later, much of the carnival was burnt to the ground after a freak lightning storm struck it, setting it and twenty poor souls ablaze. The carnival operator put it in storage, until another interested party came calling for it in 1940.

"It was shipped to Germany and put to use in a new show. One run by a Jewish family. When the Nazi forces eventually came for them—and in spite of everything else that they typically burnt and destroyed in their raids—the organ was spared, and once more put into storage. A German aristocrat purchased it after the war's end but did nothing with it; a wise move, as some would believe. It was left to gather cobwebs amidst a collection of odds-and-ends antiques, and it stayed there until the man passed, and his collection was auctioned off.

"October of 1975 saw the organ's first appearance in the United States, after it had been sold to yet another carnival, this one in New Jersey. The Stevens' Sideshow, right on the coastline. Harold Stevens, the owner, had taken on three new drifters looking for work just weeks before. They reportedly kept to themselves and saw to their games, as instructed. They were model workers until one fateful day, when they came out of their trailer hefting shotguns and revolvers and pointing them at the coming visitors. They gunned down a dozen people before police arrived, taking only one of the men alive; the second had to be put down, and the third blew his own head off before he could be nabbed. It was revealed that the men were Gerald Paige and John and Bob Hoskins, ne'er-do-wells who'd fled Texas months before, having killed a family of five for the simple fun of it. When questioning Bob Hoskins—the survivor—about their brash killing spree, he said they did it because "that music comin' out that big black sum'bitch was pissin' us off." Well, we know what sum'bitch he was referring to."

Silas stopped before the organ and finally looked at Matheson. "The organ began changing hands every now and then after that, until you acquired it from the inheritance of your late uncle, who'd bought it in 2009. Another grand collector. I'm sorry for your loss, by the way. "

Matheson kept eyeing the organ suspiciously, ignoring the condolence. "When I realized what I had, I wanted nothing to do with it. You left out a key part of the story, but I'm sure you know it. The rumor goes that the music it plays was written by the Devil himself. That it was given to Piero Vernaldi, who was instructed to build the organ so it could be played—the price he had to pay for selling his soul to the devil years before, for all his astounding talents and renown. That it and the organ are cursed, inviting disaster and driving people mad wherever it's used. "

"Oh, I know. Quite the provocative little tale, eh?" Silas gave a happy little laugh, his eyes back on the black machine.

"You must believe the story somewhat, to fork up all that money for it," Matheson grumbled, still trying to figure the entertainer out.

Silas turned to him, smiling the beguiling grin of a salesman. "Mr. Matheson, I'll hock it, I'll peddle it, I'll sell it until I have every paying customer eating out of my hands and believing in it. But I won't lap it up, myself. "

"So, all the accidents and weird goings-on that've happened around it . . . ?"

"Coincidence and misfortune."

"An awful *lot* of misfortune, if you ask me."

"Which, with the right crowds and bravado, on my part, will bring me and my troupe great fortune." Silas stepped up to Matheson, switching his grasp on his cane. He offered his hand to the scowling millionaire. "Again, I thank you for putting it up."

Matheson accepted the handshake after a hesitant moment. He looked Silas in the eye with a rather judging look. "May it serve you better than most, Mr. Goodnight."

He put his hands in his pocket and turned to leave, but Silas stopped him with a quick clutch of his shoulder. Matheson looked back to him, his slight scowl still across his tanned face. His brows arched, quietly asking what other matter remained.

"Be sure to visit my carnival, someday," Silas said in full cheer. "Reduced entrance price for you, good sir!"

"We'll see," Matheson nodded, his eyes darting back to the organ for a second. Then he turned and walked hurriedly down a row of shelving, disappearing from sight as he took a corner.

A screeching sound filled the warehouse and Silas turned back to face the nearest wall, where a steel garage door was being slid up and open. Beyond it, silhouetted by the light of the day, were two men in coveralls. A great big moving truck sat beyond them, its back end open and ready for loading.

"Ah, gentleman!" Silas welcomed them, smacking the tip of his cane on the ground. "Excellent!"

***

Norm "The AbNormal" Donahue stepped out of his trailer at the edge of the carnival, the brisk air of the October morning blowing across his tattooed skin. He paused on the top step to work up a hocker and then he sent it flying. It cleared the ten foot gap between his trailer and that of Jake "Bender" Benson's next door, striking the latter right on its screen window. Norm laughed proudly as he took the steps, his dwarfed legs taking them slowly but surely. Then he walked on towards the carnival, set to start the day's many preparations.

With four days left until opening day, there was a good deal left to see to. Being the closest thing to a right hand man as Silas Goodnight ever had, a number of duties had fallen upon Norm since he put in with the carnival, back at its onset. The tattooed dwarf was fairly business savvy, good with numbers, and could charm both vendors and investors with a well-crafted e-mail or a pleasant phone call. However, he had a reputation of being quite the bastard in person, being so crude and insulting as to incite desires to punt his diminutive self straight through a goalpost—preferably one that was miles away. Still, that hadn't ever stopped Goodnight from asking him to deal with various employees and business matters when the carnival was running.

Today's list of to-dos was no different. He'd have to visit a few out of town food vendors who'd yet to pay Goodnight for the chance to have their trucks and stands here. There were a few maintenance people to talk with about checking up on the various rides and mechanics. And he'd have to finish asking around for who'd be ready to perform in the first Mad Menagerie come opening night.

The Menagerie was a staple of the carnival, held every Friday and Saturday night for the last three years, a show where the resident freaks, geeks, and performers could strut their strange stuff and do their various acts before the 'oohing' and 'aahing' of a captivated crowd. Norm would have to ask participants what the hell they'd be doing this time around and figure out a good order for them to go in. But before he'd see to any of that, Norm wanted to check in with the boss, and he had a pretty good idea of where to find him this morning.

Norm walked past the last of the trailers and into the carnival space. Dozens of others were already up and at 'em, seeing to their tasks. A foodie was setting up a board of prices for her "Best Fried Armadillo to Ever Grace a Stick;" a gamer was stringing up prizes of stuffed bats and cartoon bloodsuckers at his Feed the Vampire water-gun game; Kristina "The Startling Swallower" Richards was hefting along a bundle of swords, any and all of which she'd stuff down her throat for the Mad Menagerie; and a heavily-pierced geek was just lounging on a bench, sticking a ten inch needle straight through both of his cheeks, apparently for the practice of it.

Jane and Hank Halston, were coming down the way and towards Norm, towering over him as they walked along on their five foot long stilts. They were already dressed in full costume, sporting dark, Day of the Dead-esque formalwear, their faces painted to look like skulls.

"Hey, Norm," Hank called down as he scooted under and between the stilts. "If you should feel warm water trickling down on you, it's not rain. Hell, it won't even be water!"

Norm sneered at the joke. He elected to stick a foot out as the stilt-walker began to take another step.

The stilt smacked his foot and jarred Hank just enough to force a holler, making him wobble for balance before sending him pitching forward. He just narrowly collided into a big bundle of hay rather than along the concrete ground. While Jane looked down to her husband, cursing Norm, the dwarf kept on walking, his grin returned to him.

He reached the Opera of the Odd, as Silas Goodnight had insisted on calling the center area of the carnival; being a great big, empty spot of space and concrete, it was a good place to have visitors crowd around and watch the Mad Menagerie out in the open. But the space wouldn't be so bare anymore, as this is where Goodnight had wanted to place that organ of his. Sure enough, Norm found both the boss and his cherished find here, a few work-hands positioning the organ and seeing to starting it up as Goodnight supervised, his cane propped up on his shoulder.

Norm stopped and stood at Goodnight's side, looking from the boss to the organ. Goodnight was smiling ever so slightly, not at all to Norm's surprise; the big ugly organ had been an obsession of the boss' for as long as Norm knew him. Goodnight had been practically giddy about this season and getting to show off his big, weird spend. Norm, however, couldn't give two shits and a flying fuck about the thing; a waste of money, as he'd tried to convince Goodnight of time and time before.

"Morning, boss," Norm said, finally getting Goodnight's attention. The boss looked down to him, giving him a proud nod.

"Good morning, Norm," he said, looking right back to the organ. It had now been properly situated, and a maintenance man had his hands in an open panel on its side, trying to get the music going. "How are things?"

"Just starting to shovel the shit. Got a lot of things to see to, but we ought to be in good pace for opening night."

"I heard you called Ms. Greene a bitch yesterday, though I never heard why," Goodnight randomly put in. Anna Greene was the carnival's resident Dog-Faced Woman, on account of her face being covered in thick brunette hair. A condition called hypertrichosis. "She was pretty upset. Came to me complaining."

"Ah, I was just trying to help her get into character," Norm giggled, not caring a fig for what the girl had to say about him.

Goodnight looked back down to him, his smile growing as he indulged the insult. "Apologize to her, all the same, when you see her again. Best to keep the peace, at least until the season closes."

Norm grumbled, knowing he'd have to find her later on to confirm her appearance for the Mad Menagerie. "Yeah, alright—I'll rub her belly and give her a treat, and all's well . . ."

"Got it, boss!" the maintenance man called out. He pulled his head out of the contraption with a grin. He flicked some switch or other, shut the panel, and waited. Goodnight held a hand out to Norm, signaling him to be quiet.

A moment of silence passed—and then the music started to play.

And it wasn't anything special.

To Norm's ears, the first little ditty it began playing was no different from any other carnival-style music he'd heard before. He'd half expected to hear some eerie dirge or an apocalyptic cacophony, after all of Goodnight's foreboding stories of it.

It wasn't at all eerie—in fact, it sounded playful—and while it was loud, it certainly wasn't bombastic or jarringly so. Norm crinkled his nose, expecting to look up to a disappointed and $10,000-poorer boss, but when he turned to him, Goodnight had a far-off look of fancy on his face.

"Beautiful," Goodnight whispered.

"Yeah, well . . . I'll leave you to it," Norm shrugged. He turned around and waddled along, wondering if his boss was finally making the slip from eccentricity to insanity. As he walked off to start his work, the music of the organ followed after him, filling up all of the carnival with its merry toots, dings, and puffs.

Goodnight stayed there a while more, listening.

***

The organ was playing another of its tunes, its tones rising and falling like a gentle wave on an open ocean. Silas' mind dipped and bobbed on its tide, letting it carry him towards a melodious horizon.

The organ was his. The *music* was his.

"Boss!" came a voice. "Hey, boss! You hear me?"

Silas looked away from the organ, blinking at the bustling, murmuring, and laughing crowds about him. Everyone from late teens to early octogenarians were milling around this busy afternoon. A silver-haired couple was just stepping off the Tilt-a-Hurl down the way, giddily chattering to each other about going right back on again. A husband was trying to win a prize at a severed-head ball toss for his obviously pregnant wife. A flock of Goth kids sat on a bench, trying to look sullen while chewing on bright pink cotton candy.

Silas had been off on a brief walk this morning, just taking in the day's visitors. When he reached the Opera of the Odd, the air filled with the loud noise of playing pipes, he'd paused to listen to the organ's song. He wasn't sure of just how long he'd been standing there, lost in the tune.

He was not the only one so entranced, as he now noticed. Several visitors stood about the organ, a studious gaze on each of their faces while others walked around them and off to other choices of entertainment. Silas had been proudly spreading word of the organ's past in recent days, barking of its supposed curse and association with the tragic to all who'd hear of it; it had garnered both big scares and heavy interest, just as he'd hoped it would, and people had since been flocking to his carnival just to see the thing.

The voice calling for him rose up again. Silas turned his gaze downwards, seeing Norm at his side, an irritated look on his small face as he fought for his boss' attention.

"I said security just had to break up another fight!" The dwarf pointed a thumb back over his shoulder. "Wasn't much of anything; two guys getting into it over some game. Had their asses tossed out."

Silas gave a slow nod. "Okay. Good."

"That's the fourth little scrap this week," Norm said, sounding a bit uncertain. "Must be something in Doyle's new Dingo Dogs everyone keeps eating—other than shit for taste."

Silas gave a small laugh. The occasional little brawl between visitors wasn't much to get worried over—there were at least two every season, guaranteed, and often over insignificant things. Those numbers had already ramped up, though, since opening day two weeks ago; two in the first week, and now five this week. Silas began wondering if taking on some more brawny security would help to head it off some.

"Well, most seem happy enough with what we've got this year . . ."

Silas looked around again, the people about him too numerous to count. Attendance had stayed strong since their first day; most years, it dropped off fast, but not this one, much to Silas' pride and his wallet's pleasure. People kept on coming, and of all ages and sorts. Still, their primary clientele were young adults, many fueled by hormones and fluctuating moods; they could make for troublesome attendees, whenever they got too riled up.

"We'll see about beefing up security a tad," Silas reassured Norm, his voice muffled under the sound of the organ's music. "Show a little more muscle; quell those tempers before they rise."

"What?" Norm hollered.

"We'll see about beefing up—" Silas started to yell. He trailed off, though, when he heard the organ give a lurch behind him, just before its music suddenly fell silent.

He and Norm looked to the organ in confusion, as did a number of other visitors; the ones who'd been standing still and listening simply blinked and moved on, their interest in the contraption now gone.

Silas' eyes narrowed in concern, and he instantly felt heat flaring under his skin, wondering if the organ had just broken down. If it had, and worse yet, if couldn't be fixed . . .

He looked at the odd, blank-faced figurine standing before the pipes, as though willing it to bring the organ back to life.

His worries were intruded upon by a man's voice nearby, rising in a high, nervous quiver. "Janey . . ." he said. "Oh, God, Janey!"

All eyes turned to the source of the voice—the man who'd been at the severed-head ball toss. His handsome eyes were wide with fear as he lifted a shaking hand and pointed at his wife's legs. She and everyone else looked down, past her belly, past her skirt, and down to her bared legs, where trickles of dark scarlet were starting to fall down the inner part of her thighs.

The woman's legs began shaking as she stumbled back, her mouth opening in mounting, slack-jawed shock.

Her knees bent as she started to fall—and then she finally let loose a wail of pain. She fell to the ground, her husband falling right to his knees at her side, grabbing and holding her as he shouted for help, other visitors about them picking up the cry.

As people began rushing to the couple and crowding about in curiosity or concern, the organ gave another lurch.

It started playing its music again, picking up where it had left off on its cheery song.

The music, the murmuring of uncertain voices, and the pregnant woman's screams mingled into one confusing din.

Silas turned to Norm. "Go call for an ambulance!" he shouted over the commotion. "And remember to get a maintenance man to check the organ again! And soon! I want it in perfect working order by tomorrow night's Menagerie, damn it!"

Norm hustled off to do as he was told, leaving Silas to stand there, looking from the organ and back towards the crowd around the poor couple—but mostly, just towards the organ.

***

When news of the pregnant woman's miscarriage finally came back to them, many at the carnival had been saddened and dismayed. It was a truly shocking and unfortunate event to behold, and many a heart went out to the unlucky couple. But, the show would go on, as the old phrase went, and the incident did not stop another surge of visitors from attending the carnival the next day; it was the night of the grand

Menagerie, after all, and people always turned out to see the strange.

When night came, the thrilling event was set to begin, if only its ringmaster would take center stage and prepare the crowd for its strange evening.

Silas shuffled his feet, drawing closer to the organ and practically ignoring the large gathering of visitors standing in the Opera, waiting for the Menagerie to start.

He listened to the music, stared at the forlorn cherubs looking down at him, and stood before the faceless figure, which looked to be inviting him to stay in the tunes for as long as he liked . . .

But he had a job to do (as little as he cared to do it, now), and he turned around, peering at the waiting crowd. Most looked to him, knowing he was about to introduce the show; but several others still had their sights on the organ, listening dutifully to the music, as he wished he could do. Even some of the freaks and performers to his right preferred to pay the organ heed, rather than focusing on their coming act.

Silas cleared his throat and worked at steeling himself.

"Ladies and gentleman," he began, just barely loud enough to be discerned through the music. He raised his arms up in slack command, his cane in hand. "I thank you for coming tonight . . . as do the rest of my creepy cabal . . . and . . . and we wish to thank you . . ."

Silas struggled to get the words out, let alone to give them some bravado.

The crowd seemed to notice, looking uncertain as they watched him stumble backwards a tad, like a direly sick man forced to lead a procession. He caught a glimpse of Norm standing amid the numbers. The dwarf was urging him to get on with it, mouthing the words: "Say it, damn it!"

"To thank you . . . with a show you won't soon forget . . . To be accompanied by . . . this wonderful music. This . . . wonderful . . ."

Silas turned back around, forgetting the crowd. He took in the organ, sitting there in all its dark glory, like a terrible king before his enraptured masses.

"*My* . . . music . . ."

He let the music claim his senses, his mind twirling and dipping with every chime and tone. His ears filled with it, to where nothing else could be perceived. His eyes grew terribly hazy and he saw nothing, but it didn't matter—because he had his music.

"*My music* . . ."

He was lost in song, and stayed lost, in a horrid blackout—until his mind finally cleared, his sight returned, and he could hear more than the organ's ditty.

He heard screams. Chocked gurgles. Meaty *thunks* and wet slashings and carnal tearing.

He was on his knees, suddenly yards away from where he had been standing before the organ, his cane lying across his knees; the blood and bits of bone upon it also coated his hands and soaked his pant legs. He swallowed hard as he blinked in growing confusion.

Then he looked about him, at the carnage that had somehow become his carnival.

The Opera was a chaotic scene of horrors. Dozens lay dead on the ground, bloodied and gutted and beaten. Visitors, vendors, gamers, and performers, alike. A few were still wrestling one another, looking to end their combatant with a solid choke or a pulling out of their eyes or by rending away at their limbs. People were darting back and forth around the stalls and the games, some simply fleeing, some looking for another victim.

A group of teens were backed against a food truck as another hacked away at them with a huge blade.

A foodie stumbled around blindly, hollering her wordless scream as she clutched at her sizzling, grease-covered face.

The famously flexible arms and legs of Jake "Bender" Benson lay yards away from the rest of him.

Kristina "The Startling Swallower" Richards sat with her back against a bench, eyes wide, and mouth open, one of the Halston's stilts shoved down her throat and into her gut.

Then there was Anna Greene, who was on all fours a few feet away, chomping and chewing away at a hole torn into the tiny torso of Norm. His tattoos were completely lost beneath the layer of red sleeked across his skin. The Dog-Faced Woman pulled away at one of his intestines and began swallowing it down.

Silas groaned, looking down and away from the sick goings-on; he instantly regretted it. Before him were four more bodies of dead people, their heads caved in and puddles of blood spreading out all about them. He let his cherished cane slip from his hands, holding his arms up and away from the dead. A weak groan escaped his lips and he felt like retching.

He began to heave out nauseous breaths, his body trembling. What . . . ?

Before he could even hope to make sense of what had occurred here, his thoughts were once again pulled away from him by a harsh sound.

The organ gave a jostle yards away and its music became muted. Silas stared at it through teary vision, listening as its high, quick tones became sluggish and distorted, falling into a dull drawl. The music murmured and drug along for a moment more, and then ceased with one last vomit of noise.

The organ remained quiet, its songs played and its work done.

The sounds of murder and the screams of the murdered were the only music left to fill the night, and as Silas knelt there, wondering at how this all could be, the distant whine of police-car sirens added themselves to the macabre movement of the night.

The Pitch

David hadn't been feeling up to doing a whole lot of anything as of late, so when his doorbell rang, he decided to just stay in bed. Whoever it was would go away after another try or two, and he could go right back to just staring at the wall in so-called peace. But after another dozen or so rings, it was obvious that whoever had come by his apartment wasn't going to give it up.

Hauling himself up, David ambled out of the bedroom and down the hall. He left the lights off, using the glow of the mid-day dimness to make his way through his unkempt, none-too-fresh apartment. As another ring died down, he opened the front door, leaning against it and heaving a sigh. A man stood out in the hall, a big smile on his taut, pale face and a dark herringbone suit and tie adorning his thin frame. He held a rather large, vintage leather suitcase before him, both of his slender hands clasping its handle.

"Good morning, sir! And how are you today?"

David gave a hesitant shrug and spoke in a hush. "Okay, I suppose."

The man gave an odd little tilt of his head and laughed through his hooked nose. "Now, we both know that isn't true, Mr. Thompson. That's why I'm here, after all."

David gave another shrug and shook his head in confusion, wondering exactly how it was that the man knew his name. "Uhm . . . I'm sorry?"

"I'm a salesman, sir, and the best salesman should know what a potential customer wants before they even come walking through the door—or me to your door, as the matter is today." The man's dark eyes lit up as he continued on with the pitch, all of that passion in the middle of his sunken sockets creating a rather hypnotic effect. "You need a keen sense for another's desires. I have that sense with you, sir, and I dare to say that I can offer you exactly what you want. Exactly what you *need*."

In spite of his lethargy, David's curiosity had been peaked. The Salesman had a way of speaking that grabbed the ear, a tone which snatched and caressed the attention. And those eyes . . .

"And what is it that you think I want?"

The Salesman blinked and held his chin out with an air of confident knowledge. He answered in that persistently pleasant way.

"You want to die, sir."

For a long moment, David said nothing. He simply stood there, thinking and observing the Salesman. Eventually, he stepped back and opened the door a little further.

"Come on in."

The Salesman sauntered along beside David as they moved into the living room. David trudged to the window, ignoring the light switch entirely. He slid the curtains open a ways, keeping the room just dark enough for his tastes while letting in some light for formality's sake. The dust in the air floated languidly about, much like David did as he crept back around the room.

He sat down in his old recliner. He motioned for the Salesman to join him on the catty-corner couch; the man shook his head and remained standing across from David, setting his suitcase on the table between them. He stood there a moment, his pale face framed within the black screen of the TV on the wall at his back. Its sheen complimented that peculiar luster of his deeply-set eyes.

He stood there for a moment with his fingers laced before him, apparently waiting for David to settle in and speak first.

"So, what exactly is this . . . all about?" David asked in a mumble.

"You, sir," the Salesman said, acting surprised at the question. "This is all about you, and the malaise you've found yourself in as of late. How do I know of this troubled state, you may ask? Well, it's just my business to know. And my business is dealing in demise. There are dozens, hundreds, dare I say even thousands of people like you around, Mr. Thompson. People who are stuck between life and a hard place, thinking their lonesome and apocalyptic thoughts, feeling as though all the world has fallen out from under them as those thoughts carry them off further and further into a dark place—and yet, all the while, they're staying right. Where. They. Are. Unmoving in motion, in thought, and in emotion. As I said, Mr. Thompson, they're stuck. *You* are stuck. I and my services—the wares I sell—can unstick you. I am offering you a simple—and, admit it—*desired* death."

The Salesman paused, letting that all sink in. After a moment, he offered his customer a chance to speak. David, not feeling much like talking, waved him to go on. The Salesman obliged, presenting his suitcase.

"Now, what I have with me in this case are rather simple things. A salesman should always be honest about his items, after all. Indeed, most can be found just about anywhere. But I am selling you more than these items—

should you be interested, of course. I am selling you an *opportunity* along with them. Those sad and solitary people I detailed? They may see these items often enough, but they do not see the proper opportunity to . . . use them."

The Salesman went quiet again, wringing his hands and looking at David—gauging him, measuring him up. Judging by the smile on his face, he liked what he saw, what effect his pitch was having.

David ground his teeth and swallowed through the dryness in his mouth, his chest bobbing shallowly. He blinked. He clasped and unclasped his hands.

"What would this cost me?"

The Salesman held out his hands, palms up in honest offering. "Each item has the exact same price. If you should purchase one, the payment is your pain. The release of your discomfort and your distress is all the remuneration I ask in my business."

Another stretch of silence followed as David considered this. Finally, he asked: "Can I see them?"

The Salesman positively beamed. "Of course, sir!"

He leaned over and set to unlatching the case. He opened it with gradual reverence, the lid positioned to where David couldn't see its contents. The Salesman looked over his items with serious consideration and then dipped his hand inside.

"How about these beauties?" the Salesman asked. He pulled out and presented a plastic bag of about a dozen or so razor blades, their edges glinting in the sunlight with a lethal loveliness. They gave little clinks as he gave the bag a showman's shake. "You can't go wrong with a classic! A strong hand and a quick swish, and all of your problems are solved."

David shook his head at this. He lifted his left arm from the couch, his hand trembling ever so slightly. He was showing off his wrist and the faint line of a scar that stretched across it. After the Salesman had a good, solemn look at it, David relaxed his arm again.

"I tried that about a year ago," he said with a flutter. "Hurt like hell, and I didn't quiet care for it."

"Of course," the Salesman said, appearing abashed at his opening presentation. "It is a bit of a nasty deed, I suppose. But don't you worry—I have a selection for you, after all."

The Salesman set the bag back in the case and flicked his fingers busily, contemplating what he had to offer. He gave an excited little sigh as he found his next push.

His lithe hands reached into the case and pulled out a long, snaking length of white rope, its end tied up in a noose.

"This one's another old-faithful," the Salesman said. He held the noose up before his face and looked at David through the loop. He let it swing to and fro in an ominous fashion. "Though I wouldn't recommend it for those afraid of heights." He gave a quick chuckle at his little attempt of a joke, but David didn't acknowledge any humor in it.

"I, uh . . . I've heard those can take a while to . . . get it done. If you don't fall just right. I'm not sure I could take that, if it didn't . . ."

The Salesman's smile fell, but only for a second. He nodded and wrapped the rope back up. "You want something a little less painful, am I right? Most do. And something quick. I suppose you wouldn't want the vial of rat poison I offer, either. Most people put it in their food or drinks and let it take effect slowly. Some even say it makes their meals taste better!"

Again, the Salesman's sense of humor didn't hit home; David just stared at him, sinking further into his chair.

The Salesman went right along talking, trying to shame the silence as he put the rope away. "But, like I said, that takes a while, and it can get rather messy and unpleasant. Now, if you want to shuffle off this mortal coil with ease, perhaps you'd like a handful or more of these?"

He straightened himself and held out two bottles of pills. One was stubby and white, the other a translucent yellow and quite large. David couldn't tell exactly what brand of medications they were from where he sat.

"These are perhaps my most popular items, and I'm proud to say that I have quite the array of colors, combinations, and quantities when it comes to these little tablets of tranquility. One whole bottle is advised for your particular usage, though more would almost certainly assure a desired end. Just take them before bed, slip into unconsciousness, and then—"

"I don't . . ." David cut in, but his words failed him and he trailed off.

The Salesman fell silent, looking at him with well-masked irritation, waiting for him to finish.

David composed himself and continued. "I've heard that those aren't always a guarantee. You can take a whole bunch and . . . still wake up."

The Salesman gave a little shrug. "Well, as I said, I have many types to choose from, and you can have all you want . . ."

"I just don't think those are for me," David said bluntly.

The Salesman's face crumbled, a sad smile being all that remained of his previous enthusiasm. He returned the bottles to the case. "I'm afraid I have only one other item left to show you, Mr. Thompson. I tend to save it for last when dealing with customers, as it tends to make them uncomfortable to see it. But, I can promise you, it is by and large the most efficient of these products."

The Salesman pulled out a Ruger GP100 revolver. He held it out gingerly, keeping its 4.20 inch barrel downwards. Its straight-black finish and grip stood stark against his pallid skin, making it look perfectly deadly. There was power in that appearance, alone. A promise of finality. David stared at the gun fixedly while the Salesman detailed it, listening to that promise that was now whispering in his head.

"If you want quick, painless, and guaranteed all in one, this is what you need, sir." The Salesman's smile returned in full as he noticed the intent gaze on David's face; his friendly, open tone picked up, in kind. "Now, when most people envision using this, they get the idea that it would be agonizing. Well, I swear to you, that is simply not true! It carries with it a connotation that is grossly unwarranted. I, personally, blame television—and all the violence shown on it—for this misconception. Indeed, this item can bring an end so instant that you do not—I repeat, *do not*—feel a thing. And as I mentioned, no item is more efficient and guaranteed in its use than this bit of steel. It comes with a single bullet, already in the chamber, as that is all you will need. Just insert the barrel into the mouth and set it directly under the roof for optimal application. Cock it, pull the trigger, and . . . that's all she wrote, as they say."

The Salesman paused, waiting for David to object again or pose a question. He did neither, his mind working matters out silently as he kept his unblinking eyes on the gun.

The Salesman inched around the table and towards David, switching his hold on the weapon and extending the grip out before him. "Would you care to hold it, Mr. Thompson? Perhaps get a feel for it?"

David looked up to him, then back to the gun. After a hesitant moment, he reached a terribly steady hand up, setting it to the grip. The Salesman let go of the gun as David pulled it close to his chest, cradling it, his eyes now staring into blank space.

The Salesman took a step back, anticipating that this deal was about to be closed to both parties' satisfaction.

David breathed in. Out. In.

His eyes were wet and wide and his nose gave the occasional little twitch. Ever so slowly, he opened his mouth and brought the gun up to his face. The ice-cold tip of the barrel slipped past his lips, stopping as it met his palate.

David breathed in. Out. In again.

He set his thumb to the hammer and brought it down. The barrel spun under his jaw, clicking the loaded chamber into place. His grip on the gun tightened. He pressed the barrel tighter against his mouth and set his finger to the trigger. It started to squeeze down oh so slightly.

David breathed in. Out. In . . .

He let his breath out in a choked-up rush as he pulled the gun away. He swallowed down hard, looking away from the Salesman as he held the gun back out to him.

"I can't . . ." he whispered softly.

The Salesman did not move, for a moment. He just gazed down at David with a disappointed look, biting his lower lip glumly. He eventually sighed and grabbed the gun, setting the hammer back down and turning away.

"Well, as I cannot do it for you, and as you aren't interested in any of the other items I have, I'm afraid that's the extent of our business today, Mr. Thompson." The Salesman set the gun back in the case, closing and latching it up once more. He rose again, lugging the case up and off the table.

David finally managed to look at him, but remained in his chair. He was breathing calmly again and gave his eyes a brisk rub. When it was obvious that he wasn't going to rise, the Salesman stepped back over to him. Reaching into the pocket inside his jacket, he produced a thin business card that was just barely whiter than his hand. He held it out to David, who timidly accepted it.

Looking it over, David noticed that it was utterly blank on both sides. He looked to the Salesman, eyebrows furrowed in confusion.

"In case you change your mind. I'm only ever a call away, for those who want to do business." He grinned and nodded, his professionalism back in swing. "I'll show myself out, now."

The Salesman turned and strode off. David watched his lanky black back as he went along, head held high and case swinging. He disappeared around the corner, his casual steps echoing across the floorboards and down the hall. As the front door opened, the Salesman called back in a cheery voice:

"And have a nice day!"

The door shut a second later, and the apartment was quiet again.

David sat there for a good while, mulling things over and over in his head. He could still feel the sensation of the gun's grip in his hand—a slight burning against the palm. He didn't stand up until it faded away, minutes later. He glanced about for a moment without really seeing much of anything.

Then he turned around and went back to his bedroom. He kept the shades open, deciding to let the light in.

He set the Salesman's card on the edge of his dresser, where it could always be in sight. He lay back down in bed, propping his head on his pillow and staring towards the dresser.

Eventually, he rolled over and managed to fall asleep.

The Four Laddies

"So, who are these guys again?" Harry Weyland asked, swatting the make-up girl's brush aside when it came too close to popping into his mouth. "The Four Chaps?"

"The Four Laddies," Gerald Dawson corrected. The executive producer laid a pudgy hand along the counter of the station, leaning his bulky frame against it with a harsh sigh. The light from the bulbs encircling the station's mirror glistened off of the man's balding scalp.

"Think they'd be insulted if I introduced them as the Four Ladies, instead?" Harry brandished that devilish grin that had gotten him on the likes of *Cosmopolitan* and *Teen Magazine*. "It's San Francisco, after all. Viewers probably wouldn't even bat an eye-lash at something like that, these days."

Dawson let out a hog's harrumph. "Ain't that the truth. Ten years in television as of next month, and the things I've seen in that time alone. I'll tell you . . ."

And Dawson proceeded to tell him, though Harry tuned out before the next word could pass his producer's lips. Harry kept his eyes on the man's fleshy dome as he prattled on, lounging back in his chair while the make-up team did their last touches. Dawson had always insisted the premature hair-loss was a direct result of the stress that came with his job, but Harry thought that a murky gene pool was more likely to blame. After all, not everyone could look as good as he did. Some people were just born with that incredible "it;" still, he reminded himself, it wouldn't hurt to get some more of that hair tonic that Sonny Bono had turned him on to.

". . . but no one wants to see acts like that anymore," Dawson was saying. Harry tuned back in, now that the rant sounded like it was nearly ended. "Now, the weirdos have taken over the airwaves."

"Speaking of which, has Bill been able to talk that rock 'n' roll woman and her band into appearing next month?" Harry struggled for a moment to recall the singer's name. "Alice Cooper?"

Dawson let his host's slip-up slide, giving a small shake of his head, instead. "Haven't heard. Haven't even seen Bill in the last week."

The Bill in question was Bill Wesley, ass-kisser extraordinaire and head booker for their weekly talk and variety show, *What's Happenin'?*

"I haven't seen him around much either," Harry grumbled. "Last I saw him was when he came to me about these Four Laddies. Found them playing in some hippie-dippy bar, or something. Made it sound like these guys couldn't be missed. He laid so much fertilizer down about how we just *had* to let them on that the expectation has even grown on me, a bit. He's got to be around here somewhere. If there *is* any credit to be had in finding these boys, he wouldn't miss that."

Dawson shrugged. "Maybe we should put out an all-points bulletin. "Missing: Bill Wesley. Booker and bull-shitter. Distinguishing features: beady eyes and a perpetually brown nose.""

After one last pat of something on his cheek, a make-up girl gave Harry a tap on the shoulder, letting him know he was good to go. Harry gave the team an obligatory smile and rose from his chair, pulling the protective papers from the shoulders of his leisure suit. He let them fall to the floor as he strode off, Dawson following in tow.

"Have you met them yet?" Harry asked, giving his plaid tie a little tug for adjustment.

"The band? Yeah. Quiet fellas, for being of the rock 'n' roll sort. Rather odd, too, if you ask me."

"Odd, huh? Well, what do you say to introducing me? I'd like to get a feel for them. Gauge how much I can razz them during the interview."

They left the dressing room and headed out into the hectic backstage area, which was alive with the threat of filming. Wife-beaters lugging equipment and interns carrying clipboards weaved out of the two men's way as they approached—some out of respect, some out of disdain masked as respect. The only soul brave enough to come up and shake their hands was David Meeks; the roguish actor was rumored to be up for an Oscar for his performance in *Sally's Secret*—the blockbuster drama of the summer—and his appearance on the show would help get the buzz to sizzling all the more. After a quick well-wishing for a good show, the mustachioed thespian went on his way, and Harry finally let Dawson take the lead.

The producer waved him over to a relatively-quieter corner of the backstage area, where four young men in gray-black suits stood in a semi-circle, hands in their pockets and eyes to the floor, silent and emotive as statues. They glanced up as Harry and Dawson approached, blank stares plastered on their youthful faces—which Harry assumed were either inherent expressions of stupidity, or the result of some pre-show, stress-relieving drug use. Harry wouldn't mind if it were the latter, so long as they could still give a decent performance; hell, he'd taken a toke and had a snort plenty of times before getting in front of those cameras.

"Gentlemen," Dawson boomed, waving a gallant hand towards Harry. "This is Harry Weyland, our esteemed host. Harry—the Four Laddies! Daniel, Clark, Paul, and Fred."

The four boys cracked weak smiles and mumbled some hesitant greetings, each nodding lightly, keeping their hands clasped before them, seeming more like somber morticians than raucous youths. Harry spared a second to analyze each one, and he just knew that he wouldn't be able to place their respectful names with their faces. The four were utterly unremarkable in just how similar their features were. Somewhat shaggy hair that hung down just above their eye-lines, their locks colored in very slight variations of brown; sharp chins; thin noses; wan cheeks; sunken eyes. Perhaps the Four Laddies had begun life as four simple brothers before picking up their instruments. Harry made a mental note to try and remember to ask them if there was any relation come the interview.

"Glad to have you on the show, boys! I'm expecting big things and a great tune from you. My booker was raving about you. Hell, he was *begging* me to let you on. Made you sound so big, you would've thought you were the Four Horsemen instead of the Four Laddies!"

The four musicians just stared at him as he chuckled lightly.

"That was a little thing called a joke, boys," Harry said, giving the nearest of the musicians a pat on a rigid shoulder. "Tends to make a person do this little thing called laughing."

The one he'd tapped gave a side-glance to the others, and they looked to him, their heads tilted down in uncertainty, like schoolboys before a judging headmaster. After another still moment, the now-de facto spokesman for the group turned back to Harry, a big smile suddenly overtaking his features. The boy's vacuous stare had been odd, but Harry found this forced show of mirth to be even odder, somehow.

"Yes, of course. Well, uhm, allow me to give our thanks for letting us appear on your show. We've been waiting for a chance like this. We think we have something special to share with your audience."

Harry gave an obliging laugh and held his hands out in a "No prob, Bob" kind of way.

"I'm happy to have you! But hey, it's just about show-time! I'll see you in a few, out there under the limelight!"

The boys gave their curt nods again, and Harry and Dawson left them to their corner.

When they were out of earshot, Dawson leaned in and asked: "So, what do you think?"

Harry shook his head and tongued his cheek, the way he always did when he was feeling rather displeased and doing his best to hide it. "I hope they're saving their voices—and their personalities—for the taping. Otherwise, the next thing Bill Wesley's booking is his own spot at an unemployment line."

A bespectacled somebody with a headset on stopped them in mid-step. "We're all set, Mr. Dawson! Ready for you on stage, Mr. Weyland!"

"Well, time to see if I can squeeze water from their stones," Harry said, smacking Dawson on the back. "Let's get this over with."

Harry headed off towards the set, stopping before the curtain that would open up and reveal him in all his hostly glory. He could hear stagehands calling for the crowd to quiet down; once they did, the show's theme music cued up and Marty Jacobs, the announcer, began his introduction from his little booth just offstage.

"It's that time of the week, folks! Time to see what's happenin' in the U.S. of A. on . . . *What's Happenin'?*! And now, here's your happenin' host, Harry Weyland!"

The crowd started clapping, and as the curtain pulled away, the cheers rose up. Harry flashed that winning smile and stepped out into the lights, the five cameras situated around the studio swiveling right onto him. Behind them were four huge sets of tiered seats, four rows each and filled to capacity with one hundred and sixty audience members looking to be entertained.

Harry took his spot on the shag-carpeted stage that bore his desk, sofas for his guests, and the Four Laddies' instruments, the latter arranged on the far left of the stage and prepped for the end performance. Harry welcomed everybody to the show, playing it up for the in-house audience and the thousands of others who'd be seeing this on their televisions two nights from now.

After his opening monologue (which included jabs at President Ford's reorganization of his cabinet and some thoughts about the wacky reception to a new movie called *The Rocky Horror Picture Show*) Harry took his seat behind his desk, introducing the night's first guest: Nicole Danes, rising star of a daytime soap opera called *Hastings' Getaway*. The young actress got a big applause from the audience, and they whistled like crazy when Harry said how he'd just love to co-star with her in a one act play of his own composition—one with plenty of action, but few lines. Harry continued to balance his half-hearted questions with his overt flirtations until the actress returned to the backstage and David Meeks came out as their next guest.

The actor promoted *Sally's Secret* a fair deal, at first, but their talk soon turned to the speculation going around about Meeks' involvement with Lykke Nilsson, the Swedish tennis star. Meeks actually turned red at Harry's suggestions of what other games the actor could play with such a woman, but Meeks left the stage laughing, and the audience had joined in the merriment.

Then, it was time for the Four Laddies to come out.

"As you all know, we like to bring big people onto *What's Happenin'?* Big people who are doing big things." As Harry started in with his segue, he looked into camera three, reciting from the teleprompter hanging over it. "But we also like to shine a light on the little people who, with some luck and talent, will be on their way to doing big things and counting themselves among those big people. With that in mind, I'd like to welcome our final guests for the evening. The Four Laddies!"

The crowd clapped as the four youths came onto the stage in procession, though the applause was much more reserved than it had been for the other, more recognizable guests. Harry took that to be a bad sign—for their ratings, if not for the band.

The Four Laddies gave the people little waves as they hurried over to the sofas, their pseudo-smiles still timid, still aimed downwards. Harry got right into his questions before the last of them could even ease himself onto his seat; the host's hopes for this closing act had already fallen to zero, and besides, he was wanting to get in another, more personal interview with Nicole Danes before the night was through—God willing.

"So, boys, first things first: what's with the name? Why the Four Laddies?"

The boys looked at each other in hesitation while the last of the applause trickled down. Another silent war of who was to speak was waged in a few quiet seconds, and apparently, the one sitting nearest to Harry lost.

"Well, because there are four of us."

The crowd laughed at that, thinking it was a bit of humor on—Paul's? Frank's?—part. But Harry was far less certain about that, wondering if the young man was just being stupidly earnest.

"Fair enough, fair enough. But why Laddies? Some alliteration could really make you guys pop! Why not the Four Fellas, or the Four Freakies? That sounds better to me!"

Laughter filled the studio again, and Harry looked out to the crowd with a grin. From off to the left, he caught a glimpse of Gerald Dawson sitting at a row of monitors and sound equipment, alongside others who were overseeing the taping. The executive producer held a cigarette between his fingers; he frowned at Harry through a haze of smoke, as if to say: "Easy, now."

As the laughter died down, and as the other band members just continued to stare, the fourth just shrugged his shoulders. "I don't know, really. We just went with that name."

Harry laughed. "Well, with profound insight like that, I can't wait to hear your boys' lyrics! So, how long have you boys been together, making music?"

The spokesman shrugged. "Not very long. Just starting off, actually."

"Oh, okay. I didn't know if maybe you started off as the Four Babies and then grew up to be laddies. Maybe you were toddlers strumming guitars and banging on drums with spoons to make funny noises. After all, that's what most rock 'n' roll music sounds like to me."

There was more clapping and more giggling and more blank stares from the band. When none of them seemed likely to respond, Harry went on, knowing the Razzy Train was a-going.

"Speaking of which, why rock 'n' roll for you boys? Why not some disco or country western? You could be wearing some nifty cowboy hats instead of those suits, you know."

"It's just what we were made to do."

Harry smiled at the boy, but there was no real pleasantness in it. Only a challenge. "Well, we'll see about that in just a minute. But I'm sure our audience would like to hear a bit more about you first. Are you boys from San Francisco?"

Another of the laddies shook his head. "We're just kinda from around."

"Okay. So where can people catch your show at?"

"We've been a few places around here. But we're hoping to take it on the road, if this show goes as well as planned. Bring our music to the whole country and all. Then the world."

Harry laughed. "Well, I wish you a lot of luck with that, boys. And with that said, what do you say to blessing us with one of your songs now? What'll you be performing for us tonight? "

"It's a song of our own and it's called "The End of All Time.""

Harry shook his head and looked towards camera two, thinking: *And just maybe the end of your career, pal.*

"That's quite the title! Well, here they are, folks! The Four Laddies, performing "The End of All Time!""

Applause struck up as the band rose and trudged over to their instruments. The lights in the studio dimmed and a spotlight switched on up above, casting the Four Laddies in a yellow-white glow as one sat down behind the drums and the others slung on their guitars. Harry eased back in his seat, grabbing hold of a pen to fiddle with as he watched a possible train wreck unfold. He gave a wry smile as the lanky lads partook in a whispered pow-wow before taking their spots and facing the audience.

The crowd went still as the boys stood there, staring down to the shag carpet. Then one of the guitarists rose his pick up over his head and brought it down, strumming out a drawn out, distorted note. He held it for three seconds and then strummed it again, and then again. As the tone drew out, the drummer began to tap out a trot against the cymbals. When he gave a beat against the bass drum, the four of them all came in, the song going off into a jaunty swing as the bass player plucked out a constant salvo of chords. The lead guitarist stepped up to his microphone and he started to sing:

"I woke up today and I was feeling great.
I got my rest; yeah, I got my eight.
I brushed my teeth and I dressed up smart,

Itchin' to get an early start."

Harry looked to the crowd as the song picked up, seeing that quite a few were already into it, bobbing their heads and patting their hands on their knees. Their mouths were slack and their eyes were riveted on the band, and Harry hated to think that, just maybe, he would turn out to be wrong; as a matter of fact, he was already tapping his pen against his desk to match the drumbeat, and his heart was thumping a tad bit harder.

"I turned on the TV and what'd I see?
Something mighty awful; said, "Woe is we!"
For the world's stopped turning and it won't go—
Go back to the way it was before.

And Mr. Newsman, well, he started to cry,
Pullin' his hair out, such a terrible sight.
He looked to the camera and this he said,
And it just won't get out of my head."

As the chorus came crashing in, all of the crowd started to rise to their feet, cheering and whooping and carrying on as though the Four Laddies were globetrotting chart-climbers instead of the young-bloods they were. Harry simply couldn't believe it, and yet somehow he could, because now his free hand was slapping at his desk alongside his pen, and his heart was running wild in spite of his still-bitter self.

""The end of all time is a-comin' today,
The wise man screams while the holy prays.
I say, the end of all time is a-comin' today.
We lost ourselves and we lost our way.""

Harry looked to his own drumming hands in disgust, willing them to stop, and yet somehow unable to do so. They had a life of their own, and now his feet were joining in, banging against the underside of his desk. The exertion—and a building dread—were starting to bring a sheen of sweat to his brow. And all the while, the music and the lyrics forced their way into his ear, the guitars sounding louder with every chord and the words growing more apocalyptic.

"Well, the truth is sad, but I can't deny
That things've gone wrong for you and I.
Invasions are in and hypocrisy's hip.
Another hard war brings another bad trip.

America's youth learn their ABC's
With alcohol, barbiturate, and cocaine dreams.
It's leadin' them nowhere, it's bringin' us down,
While disease and poverty make the rounds."

Harry's eyes shot over to Gerald Dawson and the film crew, and he was terrified to see that they were dancing and grooving in their chairs as manically as he was, and with the same looks of uncertainty and concern on their faces.

The spotlight up above began to flicker and dim, and the green, red, and orange colored lights they sometimes used began to flash on and off, casting the studio in strange hues and fleeting shadows, like some demented and erratic disco. Still, the song went on.

"God's on the dollar but he ain't around;
He's packed up his bags and he's left town.
Now, I'm thinkin' our time comes with a bomb;
So head for your shelters and try to stay calm.

The end of all time is a-comin' today,
The wise man screams while the holy prays.
I say, the end of all time is a-comin' today,
We lost ourselves and we lost our way."

At the end of the chorus' refrain, the rhythm guitarist went into a wild and sweeping guitar solo. And that's when the entire studio burst into a scene of sheer lunacy.

As the band played on, certain members of the audience began to turn upon one another, their cheering and their dancing causing them to bump and careen into each other; and the more this happened, the more wild and agitated they became at the offenders. In no time, shoving and swearing erupted into outright fist fights and throttlings between men and women alike, clawed hands scratching at faces, fingers searching for eyes, and grips going for necks with the ferocity of ancient berserkers. A strapping gentleman sent his fist flying into the nose of an old, beehive-sporting woman, who tumbled off the top row of their tiered seats, red pouring from her face. A young boy leapt from his seat and onto the back of a man who wailed in surprise, the boy trying to shove a hand into his mouth, aiming to rip out his tongue.

Others escalated the insanity of the situation with acts of apparent cannibalism, dozens of screaming mouths going for the nearest limbs available, an inhuman hunger overtaking the attackers' eyes. A young couple turned on each other, the woman sending her teeth ripping through her boyfriend's esophagus while an old grandfather in the row above them started to lose his fingers to the throats of his grandchildren. A whole gang of people on another flank of seats fell upon a portly gent standing at the bottom, sending him to the floor, going for his gut like lions would a downed and sickly elephant.

The squeal of the guitar solo came to a halt, giving way to the frenzied pounding of a drum solo. The booming and the banging mixed with the bloodcurdling screams and angry yells of the audience.

One distinctive cry rose up from off to Harry's left. He fought to control his fit enough to where he could turn about, looking back to the curtain where he made his entrances. David Meeks came falling through the veil of red fabric, a hollering Nicole Danes on top of him, wrestling him down to the floor. Meeks was trying to fend her off, but to no avail; the actress' pretty visage turned into an animalistic snarl as she shoved her face down to his, sticking her mouth across the actor's eye as she began to bite down and suck it out of the socket.

Then, Marty Jacobs appeared from behind them, turning his head about like a wolf searching for its quickly-escaping prey. When the announcer's sights fell on Harry, he came running, and in no time at all, he was leaping across the desk, hands going for Harry's neck. The two men tumbled over, Harry falling out of his seat and rolling onto the floor as he fought with Marty, his pen still clasped tightly in his right hand. They rolled about for a short bit, until Harry got the upper hand and sent the pen's tip into Marty's temple, striking out with lethal, unthinking instinct.

As Marty went still, Harry got up on trembling legs, staring out to the continuing madness.

The curtain to his left and which encircled the studio had managed to catch fire, the fabric now coated with a spreading flame that reached upwards and steadily along the rest of the curtain. It had been started by Gerald Dawson's flung cigarette; Dawson lay on the ground, quite dead, vomit pooling out from his mouth and some violent kind of sores in full bloom across his face. And he was not the only one succumbing to the rapid ailment, whatever on earth it was. Dozens of audience members were clawing at themselves as they coughed up blood and vomit and swayed about, the sores forming across their skin and still spreading as, one by one, they dropped down dead.

And while some continued their fighting, others fell back into their seats or to their knees, screaming as their skin began to mottle and rot away, their hair growing gray in seconds, the decay of ages sweeping over them in an instant. A man fell upon the stairs as his eyes bubbled and shrunk back into his head, and when his body fell, his appendages broke free from their failing flesh and his loose clothing, an arm flopping down onto the floor, lying there like a dead worm on a hot street as it shriveled up into nothing but bare bone.

And all the while, the Four Laddies faced the insane audience, and they played. They repeated the chorus twice more after the drum solo's end, and as the music swelled, it seemed that it might finally be near its end.

"The end of all time is a-comin' today;
The clock's windin' down and we're rockin' away.
I said the end of all time is a-comin' today.
Goodbye, and good night, and good riddance, I say!
Hey!"

And with that, there was one last crash of the cymbals and a thunderous chug of the guitars, and the lights in the studio went out completely, leaving all to darkness; the song faded straight out, the buzzing static of the amplifiers taking its place and the reverberation of the percussion drawing out to stillness.

After a moment, the lights sprung back on. Harry stood at his spot on the stage, shaking and looking out to the audience, which no longer fought or screamed or yelled.

They'd all gone still, staring about as though having just woken from sleep—at least, those who were still alive and standing to do so, the few dozen that they were. All others lay dead, over the seats and down the stairs and across the floors, bloodied, decayed, and silent. The only sound to hear was the crackling of the still-growing fire, which no one seemed to pay much mind, given the carnage at their feet—and caused by their very hands.

Harry felt tears of madness spring forth as he looked over to the far side of the stage, where the Four Laddies should have been standing. But they weren't there anymore. They'd disappeared when the lights went out, leaving their instruments to fall, their guitars scattered on the carpet.

The pounding of fists against metal doors sounded out from the back of the studio, along with muffled shouting. People were trying to get into the studio, the screams and the chaos of the last few minutes bringing people to see what the hell had been going on in here.

Harry was about to run for the doors, to run for help, to run for the sake of fleeing this insanity—but something kept him right where he was, his fear keeping him rooted.

It was the realization that all of the cameras were still on and still filming, and that all of them were pointed right at him.

***

After the survivors' stories of that evening were all told—and after they were all sent to hospitals for medical care or sanitariums for containment—the San Francisco police department began their hard pressed investigation into the matter. They started by looking into the two parties that remained unaccounted for in the disastrous show's production: the vanished Four Laddies and Bill Wesley, the booker who'd brought the band to the show-runners' attention.

The latter was quickly found, though no answers were turned up in doing so.

Officers went to Wesley's apartment to conduct a search into his unexplained absence of late. His home had been locked upon their arrival and there was no answer to the door, despite the fact that Wesley's car was in the driveway. When they managed to get inside, officers found Wesley's body on the floor of his kitchen, the victim of a still undetermined and seemingly rapid-onset disease characterized by extensive sores across the skin.

A coroner ascertained that he had been lying there for perhaps a week.

The search for the Four Laddies went nowhere just as quickly. Though Bill Wesley had supposedly happened upon the band performing in a local bar, all queries posed to each and every proprietor of the city's many establishments showed that nobody had, at any time, hosted such a band that fit the Four Laddies' description, nor had any musicians from the local scene ever met or happened across the young men. Also, there were no legal records pertaining to any of the four that could ever be found, across any state. Likewise, police could never locate the band members' families or their places of residence, past or present.

It was as though they had not existed at all.

To this day, each of the Four Laddies remains missing.

Little Bastard

Cassie Turpin turned her head all about, fingers in her mouth and spreading her lips open, trying to find the right angle under her bathroom light. After several sighs of frustration and dubious rotations of her head, she finally spotted what she was looking for in the mirror. Leaning closer towards her reflection, she peered into her mouth and saw that the tooth that had been giving her so much pain and trouble lately was splotched with black.

Cassie gave a woeful groan and immediately regretted it—the vibration sent a sharp jab through the tooth and set it to throbbing once more. Cassie looked at her bottom right molar for a few seconds more, taking in its chipped surface and the dark stain across its top. She pulled back from the sink and stared at her reflected self, seeing her own loathsome look of irritation and worry looking her over, thinking: *Shit . . . shit . . . fuck*.

She flicked off the bathroom light as she strode back into her bedroom. The little clack the switch made bore through her ear and straight down to her tooth and she flinched with the sensation. Then she trudged out into the hall, down the stairs, and into the kitchen. The house was still and silent, and thankfully so—the pain of her tooth was now radiating up into her inner ear, making it sensitive to every little sound. It had gotten so bad in the last hour that she was even dreading the slight creak of a loose floorboard underfoot; she was making sure to step gingerly as she set to making an impromptu icepack.

Her mounting irritation rose all the more when she opened her freezer to see a nearly-depleted bag of ice wadded up in the door's shelf. She'd motored through the bag this past week, just about every chip and cube of it going to the icepacks she'd been nursing her tooth with. The packs and their chill had given temporary relief to its spasms and pangs, but hadn't done much to rid her of the discomfort for good. Combining the packs with two little used-up tubes of Orajel and an unknown number of pain pills also hadn't ceased the tooth's endless ache.

She was running out of remedies and didn't know what else to do to help herself. So, she made her little pack and sat down at her kitchen table to think things through. She nestled her elbow on the table top and eased the pack onto her cheek, holding it there while she considered her options and thought her upset thoughts.

She knew what she ought to do, but what she couldn't bear the thought of. Ever since her toothy troubles started, the dreaded "D-word" had crossed her mind now and again: dentist. But she hated the idea of going to one. Between having to schedule an appointment around work, her loathsome views towards all things insurance, and the general horror stories surrounding the experience, Cassie wanted to save going to the dentist's as a last resort. But before she decided for certain what was best to do, she figured she should look into her troubles herself. A-Googling she would go.

Cassie rose up from the table, pulling the icepack from her numbed face; if only her molar were as blissfully numb. She turned about, trudging across the hall and into the living room. Her laptop sat on the edge of her curio table. She gingerly sat down onto her couch, curling her legs up under her and bringing her laptop to bear. Keeping her pack to her cheek, a one-handed Google search of her symptoms and the blackness on her tooth gave Cassie her own diagnosis of the situation. It wasn't promising.

According to a couple of different sites, she probably had an abscessed tooth. An infected molar. The more she read up on them, the more she hated the sound of it, let alone the possibility of having one. The name alone sounded biblical. Demonic, even. "Our name is Abscess, for we are a pain in the ass."

Seeing all the nasty and gnarly images of these things didn't help matters either, nor the fact that all of the sites recommended keeping such a tooth heated rather than cooled—the cold could only worsen matters. After reading that, Cassie had dropped her soggy icepack with a self-reproaching grumble. *Stupid*, she thought. So much for her top-notch tooth care.

After a few more clicks, websites, and paragraph skims, Cassie had had enough and shut her computer off. She gave it a disgusted toss onto the opposite end of the couch. As it bounced hard onto the cushion, it gave the couch a shake and even that slight tremor was enough to send another jab into her jaw. She winced and fought the urge to scream out her frustration.

Dentist's chairs and drill-bits loomed in Cassie's mind, and though she felt flushed at doing so, she admitted to herself that she'd have to make an appointment.

She wanted to get it over with as soon as possible, but it couldn't be tomorrow; if she tried to get off work with that late of notice, Katherine Garner—Cassie's boss—would never let her hear the end of it. The day after tomorrow would be the soonest it could be arranged, assuming

Katherine's begrudging acceptance; Cassie just hoped that she could get an appointment that soon. She'd check for nearby offices during lunch tomorrow and see about calling and arranging visit. As Cassie's thoughts turned to work, she sighed again. Trying to get anything done with the way she felt would be a tremendous hurdle and pain . . .

Cassie stopped that line of thought and stood up. She was hungry, but didn't dare to eat; she wanted to watch some TV, but worried over how the noise would hurt her ears and thus her tooth; she had some housework to see to, but who wants to do chores feeling like stomped crap? Though it was still early, she decided it may be best to try and call it a night, to get some rest and see if that brought some ease to her sufferings.

Cassie left the living room, tossed her icepack in the sink, and headed upstairs, taking them slowly and moving extra cautiously after a single step creaked, sending a needle of discomfort into her ear. With that same caution, she inched to the bedroom and lay down, leaving the sheets down; she felt her forehead starting to burn with a slight fever and didn't mind the coolness of the room to counter it. She lay on her side, resting her non-throbbing cheek on her Queen pillow.

A dull yellow glow shone through the curtains, keeping the bedroom in just enough light to make falling asleep a bit more difficult. Cassie tried to clear her mind of all worries and ignore the *whoomp-whoomp-whoomp* of her throbbing tooth. A long half-hour later, she finally managed to fall asleep.

***

No one ever accused a life in Customer Service of being a glorious occupation; people that worked in it could regale all those who didn't about all the flack and brunt of rages they took, and all the general shit they dealt with on a daily basis. Those were burdens that Cassie had grown to bear as a representative for Bolt Toys, and she normally wasn't one to complain about her work. Her toothy troubles, though, had worn her too thin today.

Cassie couldn't recall a time when she'd been happier to leave work. Today's eight hours nearly did her in; between all the rising and chattering voices in the call center, the clacking of keyboards, and having to suffer her boss' patented "pissy-face" each time she happened to trudge by Cassie's desk, there had been no shortage of irritation. After Cassie had managed to find a nearby dentist's office on the web, she'd worked up the nerve to ask Katherine for time off. After boldly entering the dragon-lady's den and pleading her case, Katherine had hesitantly granted Cassie a sick day for tomorrow. Nevertheless, it didn't prevent Katherine from showing off her great irritation at the impromptu request; so, the reviled "pissy-face" had been brought out and brandished Cassie's way the rest of the long, tiresome day.

As Cassie drove back home, she thought she knew a bit of what it felt to be road-kill. Now, stepping out of a hot shower meant to relax her, she knew what it must feel like to be *wet* road-kill; the warm waters and vapors hadn't helped at all, nor had the pain relievers she'd taken the moment she made it home.

She saw to putting on her pajamas (very carefully slipping her shirt over her head, trying not to rock the molar-boat) and then took another gander at her tooth. She stepped up to her mirror, pulled back her lips, and tried to ignore how ignorant her reflection looked. She found the right angle and stared woefully at her molar. Was it just her sour mood, or had that disgusting blackness spread further across the tooth? She stupidly considered touching it with her tongue—and then she stupidly did just that. She let out a cry as her jaw erupted in pain, and she nearly bit down on her fingers. Tears welled in her eyes.

She pulled away from the mirror and groaned as her tooth throbbed on. It felt like it was growing in her mouth, pushing against her gums and threatening to burst out like those little creeps from the *Alien* movies. And the pain was *killing* her.

Wiping her eyes, Cassie took only a little comfort in thinking: *After tomorrow, you'll be gone, you little bastard.* Because no matter how much she dreaded the idea of a root canal or extraction or pulling or whatever would need to be done, she was just ready to be free of the sucker. *Can't fucking wait to get rid of you.* As though in retaliation, her tooth sent a jabbing jolt through the side of her face. Cassie squeezed her eyes shut to fight off the feeling and went back into her bedroom.

Her stomach grumbled, but she still didn't feel up to eating. This was the second day that she'd gone without anything save water; it no doubt contributed to her poor mood and weak limbs, but she still didn't want to risk it. And TV was out of the question; she relished the stillness of her house, and she wanted to keep things quiet. So, with nothing much else to do—or at least that she felt up to doing—Cassie lay down. Scenario after scenario began running through her thoughts as she wondered what her appointment would have in store for her. She contemplated it until the sun finally fell away outside her window and she began to doze off.

Before she slipped into sleep, she sent a vindictive thought her tooth's way: *Tomorrow, you little sucker. Tomorrow . . .*

***

Pain. White-hot, stunning pain. That's what Cassie awoke to.

She gave a cry and shot up in bed out of sheer reaction, and she immediately started gagging and hacking as she swallowed down a warm, coppery glob swishing in her mouth.

Her room was dark with the nighttime. Her heart was pounding a mile a minute. She was sleeked in sweat. Her jaw was singing with excruciating agony, and as she opened and closed it, struggling to clear her throat, it radiated with another stabbing sensation. She clutched at her soggy, sweat-covered sheets as she cleared her throat, swallowing down more of the warm fluid in her mouth; she finally realized that it was her own blood.

With teary eyes, she leaned over to the drawer beside her bed and switched on the lamp, a stream of blood spilling out at the corner of her aching mouth. The sudden light was more than she expected, and she squeezed her eyes shut as another wallop of pain hit her jaw. She reached a hand up to caress her cheek, sitting back down in bed and setting the tip of her tongue to her aching molar, hoping to probe it gently. She gave it a quick touch or two before she realized her tongue was touching a bare, bloodied gum.

Her tooth was gone.

Cassie opened her eyes, keeping her tongue to her still-pulsating gums. Though her pain persevered, her tooth was indeed gone; as she swallowed down more of her bloodied spit, she wondered if she'd swallowed the tooth in her sleep—if it had somehow come loose, and then down it went. Or maybe she spat it out when she woke up and didn't realize it. But *how in the hell* could it just fall out like that . . . ?

Cassie turned her head about, looking at her sheets to see if the blackened, infected molar was anywhere in sight. But there wasn't a single pinpoint of black on her floral-print sheets. She looked back to her pillows, at the head of the bed—and saw something peculiar.

The pillow she'd been resting her head on had a thick, coaster-sized pool of blood soaking through the rose-stenciled fabric, no doubt staining the pillow right beneath it. Seeing that that much blood had somehow managed to flow from her gaping gum was sickening to Cassie, and quite odd; but odder still was the thin line of red leading from the circular stain and down the pillow, a streak that crept right over the pillow's edge. Craning her head to look at the pillow, Cassie saw that the streak didn't end there; the line of drying blood extended across her bed sheet, a full foot away from the pillow and leading right over the edge of the bed. Like a line of slime left by a slow-crawling slug—only with Cassie's blood, in the slime's stead.

Confused, and feeling more blood welling up in her mouth, Cassie tossed off her sheets and made to get out of bed and head to her bathroom to rinse. She'd slipped her legs over the bed, her feet touching floor, when she heard a sound. It was quiet, but rising some—a *scritch-scratch* sound of something crunching and grinding.

She looked to the floor, and that's when she saw it.

A black mass lay plopped on the hardwood, a pile of something as big as a Great Dane's droppings and disgustingly similar in shape. What was worse, it was *moving*. By the light of her lamp, Cassie saw that the stuff was pulsating like a heart's beat and wiggling to and fro like a turtle trying to right itself. That *scritch-scratch* noise was coming from it, and it became louder as the pile began to form into something else.

As it kept rocking about, five stubby bits began to stretch out from it, and the pile began to rise up like a worm sticking its head out of the dirt. It then stood on two of its nubs— its legs—and bared its others—its arms—up over the final nub—its head. In a matter of seconds, it looked like a hunchbacked gingerbread man. And through her stunned disgust, Cassie realized that the blackness looked rather familiar to her; it looked like the gunk that had been on her tooth.

As the thing grew tiny little fingers and slowly grew in height, now standing about a foot tall, it turned around to face Cassie. Imbedded in its chest, around the relative spot where a person's heart would be, was a bump of white jutting out from the rest of its body—Cassie's molar. The creature's little face gazed up to Cassie, who sat still on the edge of her bed. Its eyes weren't so much eyes as they were little indentations in its small head, and its mouth cracked open in a jagged, tiny maw.

The thing crouched, as in defense, and took a step forward. Then it screamed at her, letting out a pig-like squeal of a war-cry. And then it came running at Cassie.

Cassie finally moved, giving a quick scream and jumping off the bed, trying to get out of the thing's path. But it was quick. It leapt up with another squeal and grabbed hold of her bare right leg, its fingers digging into her calf. Its small black body felt wet against her skin as it hugged tightly to her leg, letting out wild huffs of little, ragged breaths.

Cassie started doing what looked like a terrified tap-dance as she tried to shake the crazy thing off of her, but it held fast, its fingers piercing into her skin and drawing beads of blood. As she screamed again, it reared back its head and brought its tiny jaws clamping into her leg, making ravenous grunts as it bit away at her shin. Cassie's flailing went up a notch and she spun about, kicking her right leg out with a determined cry. Her shin and the strange creature smacked up against the frame of her bed with a hard smack. Cassie's leg erupted in pain—from the bites, the scratches, and the kick—but the thing finally let go, falling to the floor with a pained grumble.

Groaning, feeling her head spinning from shock and disbelief, Cassie turned and started to make her way out of the bedroom and into the hall. She wobbled on her injured leg, though, and her escape was much slower than she yearned for, practically hopping away as she dragged her hurt leg behind her. She'd only made it to the door when she heard the creature give a wet snarl from behind her and then felt its hands clawing away at her left heel. Though small, its fingers were like blades, and they cut fast, hard, and deep into her Achilles. With a pained holler, Cassie fell forward and out into the hall.

She landed hard on her stomach, knocking the wind out of her. The pain of her jaw was now contending with the pain in the rest of her body. Still, her fear and instinctive urge to flee trumped her discomforts, and she started crawling away down the hall. Her wounded ankle flopped behind her, and she could feel it leaking blood out onto the floorboards.

She let out strained breaths as she belly-crawled away, not sure of where she was going or what she would do to defend herself from this impossible little thing that was attacking her—just knowing that she had to get away. She'd just reached the stairs leading down to the first floor when she heard another screeching battle-cry from behind her, and then the noise was directly in her ear; the thing had launched itself into her back, and it was now clawing at her arms and her back and her neck. She tried to smack it away, but as she pushed herself up to bat it off, she misjudged her own strength and her positioning on the landing. With a jolt of surprise, she sent both herself and the thing tumbling down the stairway.

She screamed and the creature screeched as they both fell head over heels, rolling and somersaulting down the dozen or so steps. Cassie felt her shoulder smash into the edge of a step as her legs went over her, and she caught sight of the creature letting go of her shirt as it went flying; her eyes squeezed shut as she tumbled the rest of the way down.

She landed on her back with a smack at the foot of the stairs, her legs draped over the last few steps. She groaned and tears started to fall as she just laid there a moment; then she lifted her arms and arched her back, trying once more to get away.

The creature hopped back into view, giving a cackle as it landed on her chest like a pirate boarding a besieged vessel. Its limbs continued to crack and crunch as it grew larger, now an extra inch or two taller than before. It grabbed hold of her right forearm and sunk its teeth into her skin. Cassie gave a choked cry and brought her arm swinging down, slamming the creature into the floor. It let her go, and before it could get back up and keep up the attack, she swatted it away a few feet down the hall.

Cassie rolled back onto her stomach and started crawling, just barely able get her knees up from the pains of her fall. She panted as she started towards the kitchen, the nearest room in the house that could maybe have a weapon or anything at all to fight off this maddening little bastard. She heard the thing's feet scraping against the hardwood floor behind her and urged her arms to carry her on faster. She slid into the kitchen and its cool tiles, making her way to the nearest counter and its drawers full of odds and ends. There was a hammer in one of them. If only she could get to it . . .

The black tooth-creature came at her again, popping up beside her face and raking its claws against her cheek and arm, trying to get its head in between her shoulder and sink its jagged teeth into her neck. Cassie gave an angry cry, grabbed hold of one of its legs, and lifted it up. It squealed and struck her hand, fighting for freedom. Cassie heaved it across the room and it landed a few feet away, its rough body screeching against the tile.

Afforded this window, Cassie mustered up the rest of her strength and pulled herself up to the counter. She sat herself up, leaned against the bottom of the counter, and reached blindly up to the drawer, keeping her eyes on the creature. It was getting up slowly, shaking its little head in a daze. She floundered for the drawer's handle as it turned to her, sneering. Right as it started to charge across the floor, hopping along, she pulled open the drawer, pulling it right off its rollers, sending it and its contents scattering on the floor. She looked down to the mess and found the hammer. She grabbed it and whirled back to face the creature.

Right as it was about to jump up into her lap for another attack, she brought the hammer down on it. It squealed in pain as it fell to its stomach and started kicking like a baby in a tantrum. Cassie wasted no time; she kept on bringing the hammer down, smashing it again and again into the little bastard's body, some of her wild shots striking the tiled floor instead of the creature. The smacking of the hammer mixed with the pained shrieks of the little monster as bits and chips of its black body burst into the air with every strike. One of its arms flicked across the room as it broke off, and one of its legs followed quickly after that. Even after the hammerhead pummeled the things head into oblivion, ending its screams and its thrashing, Cassie kept bringing her weapon down. She didn't stop until the last of its little torso, along with her molar stuck in its chest, exploded with one final hit.

Panting, her mind and body still lost to adrenaline, Cassie let the hammer slip out of her hands; it landed in her trembling lap.

She swallowed down more bloody spittle as she shook and twitched from her pains and her prevailing fear. Her mind grasped for understanding of what the hell just happened and came up with zilch for logical explanations.

She ran a hand through her hair, trying to bring sense to something senseless. She stared at the scattered bits of the tooth-creature and she started to cry again.

Then, through the many discomforts and sensations that had swept over her, Cassie felt something that made her blood run cold. Her upper left canine started to throb with a familiar ache—just like when her molar had started giving her troubles a week ago. It was subtle, but clearly there.

She could have sworn the tooth twitched in her gum, a little tick that set it to clacking against its enamel compatriots. Then her lower right incisor started doing the same.

Cassie moaned in trepidation and saw the vicious attack from the strange creature in her mind's eye all over again. How it had nearly killed her.

She looked down at the hammer in her lap, then to the remains of the little creature. Then, she saw something among the strewn items from the drawer. She stared at it nervously, an idea forming in her head that seemed so terribly crazy. But was it any crazier than what had just occurred? Any more wild than a little demon-thing being born from her tooth and trying to kill her, for God's sake?

After a quick minute of debate, and as her teeth continued to adopt their aches, she decided it may not be so crazy after all.

***

Cassie's next door neighbor, Mrs. Carlyle—an octogenarian and insomniac—had been awake at the time the screaming and ruckus started up from the next house over. At first, she thought that the hollering was coming from a crazed crowd member on the rerun of *Match Game* that was on her television. When she finally realized it wasn't, she became worried and called the police to inform them of the late-night disturbance.

When two officers arrived on the scene some ten minutes later, they'd rang the doorbell and called out repeatedly for someone inside to answer; after nobody did, they kicked open the door with guns drawn and flashlights on and out before them. They stepped into the house with caution and started searching for signs of trouble, one of the officers giving a quick look into the kitchen before calling the other one to his side. They shined their flashlights onto Cassie, who was still sitting on the floor with her back to the counter. At her side were the miscellaneous items of her drawer, spread out among the smashed pieces of black that the officers mistook for rocks of some sort. There were dents and cracks in the tiled floor about her outstretched legs, with specks of something white scattered around them. A hammer and a pair of pliers sat in her lap. The officers were stunned to see that, along with the cuts and bite marks on her legs and arms, the front of her shirt was covered in a spattering of red, and her chin was absolutely coated with it, as well.

But what shocked them most of all was when Cassie turned her eyes up to look at them, and she gave them a wide, bloody, and completely toothless grin—right before she started to laugh and cry all at once, her mind nearly as gone as her teeth.

Chirp

Chirp.

Ron ground his teeth, his jaw going rigid with irritation. He glared up at the shadow-covered ceiling, boring holes of anger into the darkness. He flared his nostrils, breathing out more and more forcefully through them, blood pressure be damned.

Chirp-chirp.

A grumble tickled his throat as his jaw clenched ever tighter. He flexed his hands, fanning the fingers out before digging the nails into his palms, his bed-sheets wrenching between his fingers. Their tiny bones and knuckles clicked and popped under the pressure, carpal tunnel be damned.

Chirp.Chirp-chirp.

Ron growled, raising himself up a little in his too-big, king-sized bed. He rolled over onto his side, grabbing hold of his pillow and jerking it out from under his head. He slammed the pillow over his face, palm pressing the cooled pillow over his ear to try and shut out the noise. The constant noise. Even with his ears covered, he could hear the chirping of the cricket outside echoing in his mind.

Chirp-chirp chirp-chirp chirp-chirp, like the world's most irritating, tiny heartbeat.

This was what Ron Davies' summer nights had devolved to: fruitless attempts at restful sleep, steady bouts of anger, and crickets. Minuscule creatures, maximum irritation. Jiminy fucking crickets. It was peculiar how he'd never even seemed to notice them in past summers. He couldn't recollect them being so abundantly present. At least, not before Harriet had passed.

Maybe they just hadn't been around as much back then. Or maybe having had someone to sleep beside him, make love to, or even argue with took his attention from their incessant noise-making. It could easily be so; he'd come to notice a lot of different things and changes since assuming the status of widower four months ago. How much more quickly dinners were eaten when cooking for one, and the subsequent dishwashing that followed, simplified with only a single plate to scrub. How much more slowly it took the sun to fall in the western sky when no one was there to see it crawl down the horizon with you. How the littlest, most insignificant of inconveniences could drive you up the wall and around again.

How god-damn noisy crickets could be.

Since June flipped by on the calendar a week ago,

Ron had been living with the stupid little insects and their midnight concerts each and every evening. With the lone bedroom of their (his, now—he still thought if it as theirs, even with Harriet gone) one-story home situated right beside the backyard, he was sleeping next to Insecta Central. Well, *would* be sleeping next to it, if the act of sleeping were technically involved at this point. Which it wasn't, and rarely had been this whole week. What winks did come to the sixty-five year old retiree were only from sheer exhaustion and passing out at three or four in the morning, only to wake up at seven (or eight, if he won the Power Naps lotto that morning).

So, he wasn't getting much sleep, and his demeanor showed it.

It was driving him crazy.

It was getting hot underneath the pillow now. His skin prickled with heat, half from the lack of air under the linen, half from the anger simmering within. He hazarded an opportunity to lift the pillow up, holding it up momentarily, waiting—praying—to see if the chirping had ceased.

Chirp-chirp.

Ron gritted his teeth and growled once more, flipping over on his other side and slamming the pillow back down on his head.

***

The next day was as unremarkable as most. Ron woke at a quarter after seven (he'd had a few matching numbers on his lotto card, it seemed), watched some bad daytime television, read some of a Nathaniel Hawthorne novel, went for a walk around the suburbs, missed Harriet some more, ate a frozen TV dinner, and watched some bad nighttime television.

His night began with the now typical tossing, turning, and cursing of crickets. But then he managed to fall asleep. And he dreamt.

He was at the cemetery where he'd buried his wife. The sky was cloudless, yet cast in a dull gray hue. So were the trees around the graveyard and the grass underfoot. He stood before Harriet's grave, the dark gray granite of her tombstone terribly familiar to him. White wooden folding chairs arranged in three long rows were set up to the side of her eternal resting place. Human-sized crickets sat in them, bodies facing the grave, but heads turned towards Ron. Their mandibles moved in silent, scolding fashion. They were staring at him with their bulbous compound eyes and chirping silently. They weren't there to mourn with him, he knew that, they were there to laugh at him. To chirp at him.

Beside this congregation of giant insects, a band of violinists were playing. The musicians were also human-sized crickets, only these wore fancy black tuxedos over their slim, greenish-yellow limbs. They played a string-rendition of Beethoven's Moonlight Sonata, their chirps still audible over their playing, blurring with the music until violin and chirps were one.

As he opened his mouth to scream, to tell them to leave and let him be, a flood of tiny young crickets came spilling out of his mouth, and his cries became the incessant noise of the insects . . .

Ron awoke, sweating and blood boiling. He feared there really were insects in his mouth; he could feel them in the back, itching and scratching with their legs and their antennae. But it was just his throat clenching, dry and gasping for air.

He sat up in bed, propping himself up on numb arms, hitching in breaths. He felt a wet spot on his sheets, just above the stomach. He could tell by the sensation and the bitter hint of smell that he'd urinated a little in his sleep, be it from age, his dream, or a bit of both. Any shame of this came second to the sense of alarm that still gripped him in the wake of the nightmare.

My god, he thought, *my god . . .*

Those two words repeated in his mind until he heard the sound again. The *chirp-chirp chirp* from outside.

Ron's already heated blood rose a few more degrees. *Those little fuckers.*

He kicked the covers off, slamming a fist into the mattress out of sheer distress, the springs inside echoing from the blow. Then they clinked and sprung together as he lifted himself over the side of the bed. With a grunt, he got to his feet, moving quickly over to the window of the bedroom. He slid the drapes aside and stared into the night. It was dark out, but a little glow from the moon illuminated the backyard some. He saw the Merrimans' wooden fence off to the left, bordering their backyard, and the rows of trees both to the right and dead ahead that served as limits, separating his yard from the Spencers' place behind his condo and Mrs. Spitowski's to the right.

The grass was a spotless sheet of dark blue in the evening's light, but still he scanned it closely, as if he could spy the crickets that were making their noise out in the grass.

"You little shits," he whispered with hate. "You little fucks."

He rapped his hand against the window, like you would if you were trying to shoo away a pesky squirrel at your bird-feeder. The crickets kept on chirping. He hit the window-pane again, a machine-gun patter of knuckles on the glass. No luck. The crickets wouldn't relent.

Ron let out a string of curses as he moved to his dresser-drawers. He slid a drawer open and pulled out clean underwear. He slipped his dirty ones off and put on the new ones. Then he stripped his bed-sheets from the mattress. Still cursing, but in a calmer, mumbling way, he left the bedroom and threw the soiled sheets into the laundry room's washer. With that done, he trudged into the living room. He sat in his worn recliner with the lights off, flipping through useless infomercials on the television until he nodded off in his chair.

When he woke in the morning, his body was stiff from sleeping in the chair, but at least he'd slept without any more dreams.

***

Ron had resolved to get rid of the crickets.

And he had a simple way to do it; an old fashioned, tried and true way. He wouldn't have to pay for any sprays or spreads that killed your lawn with chemicals and that shit. Killing pests was good; killing pests cheaply was even better.

An old practice and home remedy that his parents used to employ would do the trick. He remembered now how those summers of his pre-teen years had been so terribly hot and humid, and how they'd brought the crickets and all other sorts of creepy-crawlers around the Davies household. He'd been enlisted, along with his older brother (now dead of prostate cancer, God rest his soul), to set out little jars that had once contained honey, jams, and jellies all around outside. Now, though, they had a concoction of death and demise for bugs in them. A brilliantly simple combination of water and molasses. Ron's mother had explained to him that the sweetness of the molasses would attract all the deplorable pests into the jars, and once they were in there, they'd get stuck, drown, and die.

Those two or three summers and their little traps had to have put a hefty dent in the insect population on the block. Each day they checked the jars, finding flies, stick-bugs, even a few small spiders now and again. And, yes, crickets. Then they'd clean the jars out, put more of the liquid in, and repeat the process. Fill them, and they'll come. And drown.

Feeling confident, Ron scouted the kitchen for old, otherwise useless jars or suitable containers. Harriet had sometimes kept such items after they'd cleaned out the food in them, on the chance they could be useful; bless her heart. In the cupboards, Ron found a Smuckers jar and a Land O' Lakes butter container. These would have to do. He sprayed some water from the kitchen faucet in each, set them aside, and hoped to find some molasses in the pantry. A ten minute search and rearranging of goods brought up an unopened bottle of the dark brown stuff.

Grinning ear to ear, he spurted some molasses in the jar and the butter container. Then he grabbed each and went outside through the back door, stepping off the patio and onto his lawn. He placed the jar a few feet from his window and the container a few feet out from the jar.

He stood back and surveyed the lawn and his traps like an army general ordering the placement of land-mines in a coming confrontation. He crossed his arms and grinned a little bit more.

"What on earth are those all about?"

The woman's voice came from behind him, making Ron jump at the ridiculously cheerful-toned question. He didn't have to look to know who it was. That high-pitched, nasal drawl unique to old biddies and practicing gossips belonged to Mrs. Spitowski.

He turned to face her and put on a fake smile. "I've got some crickets, neighbor. Looking to get rid of them."

Mrs. Spitowski, sitting on her patio's glider and sporting a nightgown, waved the remark off with the knowing gesture of a know-it-all nag. "Got to do more than that to get rid of those boogers. You'll need heavy-duty sprays and the like. Better off just buying some ear muffs to wear while you sleep, or learn to ignore them."

If I could learn to ignore them like I ignore your

advice, you old bitch, I'd be set, Ron thought. His fake smile became a little bit real at this internal comment.

He turned and made his way towards his backdoor, not wanting to get caught in conversation with the octogenarian. "I'll see how this works first."

She snorted. "Sprays or ear-muffs."

Ron stepped inside and slammed his door, not without some satisfaction. He didn't have to listen to Mrs. Spitowski anymore. Maybe he wouldn't have to hear the crickets anymore, too.

***

He heard the crickets all that night. He hoped at least a few were feeling a hankering for molasses.

***

Ron checked his traps the next morning. What he found wasn't too invigorating.

The jar was empty, save for the concoction and two flies, drifting dead in the sugary water.

The container, meanwhile had been overturned. The water and molasses had spilt out on the ground, only a tiny bit of the stuff left in the container. This surely was discouraging, but it wasn't what really shocked or upset Ron.

When he had moved to check the container, he saw something perched on its side. As he got closer, he realized what it was.

It was a cricket.

"You little shit," Ron had mumbled, perplexed and plenty pissed.

It sat there, a light green against the red and yellow of the Land 'O Lakes. It sat motionless, utterly quiet, facing Ron. It almost seemed to be looking up at him. Taunting him.

Ron had sprinted forward, foot coming down on the container. The cricket leapt away before his foot was even off the ground, though, and the plastic snapped and crunched under his loafer. He hadn't seen where the bastard jumped to; if he had, he would've gone for another stomp.

He heard a titter from behind him. He spun to see Mrs. Spitowski standing in her patio, watering her flowers. The dentures in her mouth were displayed in a broad smile.

"No luck, huh?" Oh, how irritating that nasal tone was . . .

Ron shook his head, not to respond to her question, but out of a loss as to what else to do. He squeezed his hands into fists, then reached down for the squashed container, then for the jar. He tossed the contents of the latter, then went back inside his house.

He wondered how much pesticides and that sort of product went for at Wal-Mart. It didn't really matter. Whatever the price, he'd pay it.

***

"Sprinkle contents alongside your house, no more than four feet out." *Bullshit. Don't these assholes know crickets are all over the yard?*

Ron stood in the aisle of the store, having perused all the pesticides, sprays, and spreads offered. None of them sounded too promising, like the instructions of the one he was holding. What good would a four foot area of cushion do you, even if the product worked and did kill the insects in that particular area? Crickets could be all over his yard, and the noise they make carries, damn it.

Ron shoved the bottle of spreading stuff back into its place on the shelf. He looked up and down the aisle for an employee to ask for help on what would work, but none were around. Them and cops, never around when you needed them. Sighing, he picked up a green bottle of some spray which had directions that made some amount of sense and was priced high enough to potentially be worthwhile.

He made his way down the aisle, avoiding the hustle and bustle of the shopping families about him. Flustered wives looking for dinner possibilities, husbands pushing to go to the automotive sections, children whining for candy, toys, or good old attention from everyone around them.

Like Dr. Seuss once wrote, all the noise, noise, noise.

Getting to the front of the store, Ron scanned for a relatively short checkout line. Most were packed, but he found one that looked reasonable and got in line. The twenty items or less checkouts were pretty bare, but he'd learned that fewer items didn't mean quicker ringing up. Another change he'd found in shopping for one, since Harriet's death.

As he got closer to the cashier, he started hearing the chirping.

It came seemingly from nowhere, the patented screech of his insectile enemies. *Chirp. Chirp. Chirp.*

Ron looked at the ground on instinct, expecting to see a dozen or so crickets on the store floor. A lost penny and a crumbled gum wrapper were there, but no insects. As he looked up, the cashier caught his attention. Each time she swept the bar-codes of the items across that electronic red sensor, the chirps rang out. *Chirp. Chirp. Chirp.*

It was the checkout that was making the noise, but it

didn't sound like the typical beeps that they usually made. Then he realized the checkouts beside his were making the same sound.

Each chirp resounded in his head, making him dizzy with sensory input, the drone of the chirps going on and on and . . .

"Sir?" It was the young cashier. She stared at him nervously, like he was either sick or crazy. Maybe a bit of both.

It was his turn to check out. He gave a wan smile, stepping forward and handing her the bottle of spray. He winced as she swept its bar-code. *Chirp.*

"Seven eighty-five," the girl said, bagging his purchase. He handed her a ten, the wait for change almost agonizing as the noise continued to rise around him. When she handed it to him, he snatched it out of her hand and shuffled quickly out of the store.

In the parking lot, he passed a middle-aged woman carrying a little baby girl dressed in a bright pink dress. The girl, who was drooling and jibber-jabbering as babies do, looked at Ron, smiled, and chirped. He turned his eyes away from the child, feeling a terrible need to whip out the bottle in his bag and spray the kid with it.

Chirp. Chirp. Chirp-chirp.

***

When he'd finished spraying his backyard, the bottle of pesticide was half empty. Ron had been liberal with his application of it, saying to hell with instructions. He was a man on a mission.

He spritzed the stuff all over, along the edge of his house, at the edge of the Merrimans' fence, around the somewhat existent border of the Spencers' and Mrs. Spitowski's, and all in between. By the time he was satisfied (as close to satisfied as he was capable of, anyways), his hand ached and throbbed from squeezing the nozzle of the bottle.

Now, after a dinner he just barely picked at and hours of staring at the television without really listening or watching, he lay in bed. His sheets were clean again, soft and cool around him, relaxing. Still, his body was tense with anticipation. It had been about a half hour since he called it a night, and he'd yet to hear a cricket. He waited, anticipating the first chorus of irritation to rise up at any second.

Any second, he thought, *any minute. They're out there. I know they are. I'm waiting. They're waiting.*

He rolled onto his back, wadding the tops of his covers in his hands. The night was a far cooler one than recent evenings had been, but a sheen of nervous sweat glistened along Ron's brow.

Oh, yes, they're out there. Bastards. Fuckers. They know what they're doing to me. They know. They . . .

He sneered into the darkness. Maybe the stuff he'd spread could kill them. Snuff out their pesky little existences. Wipe them out like a nuclear strike, greeting those that came next summer with a radioactive, wintry wasteland. A wasteland where they desperately fought and scrounged for whatever those tiny pests ate, like rejects from a Mad Max film.

If it didn't work, there were other ways. Had to be. He could get a new lawn mower, one with keen blades and a hunger for grass and insects. *Chirp-chirp* going to *chop-chop* as the bastards were spit out of the mower. Or he could burn them. Set his grass on fire and smoke the turds out, melting their arthropod limbs off. *Try jumping away when you're toasting quickly into nothing.* And screw what the neighbors would think; it was his property, his yard, and he could light it up if he wanted to . . .

I'll get them. One way or another. I'll get them. They won't get me.

An image from his nightmare came to him. The graveside collection of giant crickets glaring at him, eyeing him, measuring him up.

Won't get me. Never.

Chirp.

He didn't know if it was his imagination or if a cricket had really voiced its presence just now. He swallowed hard, breath rushing in and out of his nose, a V-8 engine of imminent rage revving up.

Chirp-chirp-chirp. Chirp-chirp.

NO! GO AWAY! FUCKERS!!! KILL YOU!!!

He threw the covers off, smacking his mattress like a child in one hell of a tiff. Without really realizing what he was doing, he slid his slippers onto his feet and rushed out the bedroom.

I'LL KILL YOU!

Dressed only in a t-shirt, his boxers, and his slippers, Rob yanked the backdoor open and stepped outside. Growling and snarling, beside himself with frustration, he began stomping on the grassy ground. He slammed his feet down one after the other, as a mean giant storming through a human village in an old fairy tale would. He looked like the world's most pissed off square-dancer, leaping and stomping and carrying on to a song only he could hear.

SQUASH YOU! STEP ON YOU! KILL YOU!

He made his way around his yard, growing weary and achy quickly, but endeavoring to persevere in his manic, hopeful killing spree of insects. No matter where he stepped, no matter how much noise he made, the chirping of the crickets continued.

BASTARDS! KILL YOU! KILL . . .

"What in Sam Hill are you doing, Davies?"

Mrs. Spitowski came bustling out her backdoor in her usual nightgown, interested enough to interrupt his cavorting, but not enough to hazard getting close to him as he stopped prancing about. Her face was furrowed in displeasure and judgment.

"I thought some madman was out here lurking about, hearing you carry on like you are!" She looked him up and down, that haughty sneer growing stronger as she took in his version of sleepwear.

Ron just glared at her as she went on.

"For God's sake, Davies, what's going on? Are you drunk? Are you on drugs? Should you be? People are trying to sleep you know. Not all of us can afford to dance and jive at midnight, thank you very much."

She kept at it, and so did the crickets out here with them.

"You were never that friendly to begin with, Davies, but since your wife passed, you've been downright brash and progressively odd. Grief may hurt, I know, but get a hold of yourself! If that's what's bothering you so much you should chirp. Chirp-chirp chirp. Chirp chirp chirp chirp."

Mrs. Spitowski's words skipped away and became the noise of the crickets. She didn't even act like she was aware of the change. She just kept making noise. Ron sneered back at her, thinking: *She's one of them. I see now. My dream. The giant crickets. The human-sized crickets. They are real. Human-sized crickets hiding among people, driving us crazy.*

He moved towards her as she chirped on. Her face shifted into a look of concern as he approached, but she stood fast as she continually berated him. Then another thought struck him.

She'd warned them. She saw me put the traps out the other day. She's one of them and she told them and they knew not to fall for the trick. She may even be leading them, orchestrating them against me. She's one of them.

"Chirp?"

Ron rushed the old woman, pushing her down to the ground. A single, piercingly loud chirp escaped her lips—*mandibles*—and she fell on her back. Her hair—*antennae*—tumbled around her face, obscuring it as she lifted her arms to blindly fend him off. But he was on top of her in an instant, hands around her throat and choking the insectile life out of her. She choked on her chirps as he throttled her, helpless to his anger. Her—*compound*—eyes bulged up at him, seeing his twisted face until they saw no more and she chirped no more.

He'd exterminated her. But the din of the other crickets continued.

A deep, echoing chirp sounded from behind him. Ron turned and saw young Mr. Spencer, his backdoor neighbor, moving towards him.

"Chirp! Chirp chirp-chirp!" he said, looking horrified. *Him too!*

Ron jumped back to his feet and lunged toward Spencer, ready to squash another of the bastards. He roared a battle-cry of determination and reached for the young man's—*insect's*—neck.

Spencer threw a fist at Ron, hitting him square in the jaw and knocking him out cold.

The chirping around him gradually faded away as he fell unconscious. It turned out to be the best rest he'd had all week.

***

Ron was happier than he'd been in a long, *long* time. He'd been sleeping so much better since the move to his new place. The sedatives they gave him did the trick real well, knocking him out better than a warmed cup of milk possibly could. He easily got his eight hours of sleep a day, sometimes more.

On top of that, the food here was so much better. No crappy TV dinners for him anymore. No, sir. He'd never realized how fantastic apple sauce could be until he'd tried this place's version of it. Not to mention all the other food—delicious! Pre-cut and ready for him, nary a knife or fork in sight, relying upon that devilish invention of the plastic spork for his meals, instead.

And his neighbors! So much better than his old ones. They kept mostly to themselves; Mrs. Dunlap was catatonic, after all, so she never spoke or harped him about his habits, and young Mr. Jacob Crane rarely did anything more than stare blankly into space, perhaps occasionally mentioning that his parents were set to visit soon, or another friend of Crane's that Ron never personally saw. A quiet lad, a pleasant lad. Such wonderful neighbors!

Perhaps best of all was this: his room was way up on the fourth floor, and the parking lot was just below. No grass for the crickets to make a home in.

His new place was not without its drawbacks, though. He had to visit with his new doctor now and again, which could be a pain. To talk about his anger issues. To discuss Harriet, whom he still missed terribly. The crickets.

On the last subject, Ron rarely spoke in depth with his doctor. His doctor had a kind enough smile, a genuine look of interest during their talks, and looked respectable enough in his wire-rimmed glasses and tweed jackets with the badges on the chest.

Every now and then, though, when the doctor reflected on what Ron had said, lending his opinion on matters, his voice slipped. He'd say, "Very good, Ron. Now, why do you chirp that way?" or something of the sort; a word would be replaced by that most irritating of sounds before Doc lapsed right back into English, without a pause.

Sure, the doctor seemed nice, but Ron wasn't entirely sure if he could be trusted. *They* may still be after him, monitoring him, measuring him up for whatever deeds they had planned.

They were *always* around.

Leaving the Lasso

Ray took another swing of Coors as he paced in front of his bed.

He was still dressed in yesterday's clothes. He hadn't bothered to strip out of them—or even kick off his boots—when he made it home last night. He'd passed out before he got the chance, something he hadn't done since his hard-hitting, pre-drop-out days.

His work-shirt was sour with sweat and spilt spirits, and his Duluths scuffed lines into his carpet, tracking clumps of dried mud through the shag.

He couldn't stop thinking about the kid he'd hit last night, or about washing the blood off the front of his Ford this morning.

As he turned about for the hundredth time, he looked at himself in the mirror set into his closet door. There were circles under his eyes and his scruff seemed a half-inch thicker than yesterday. Frankly, he looked like shit. He looked guilty.

He'd need to get it together, and quick.

At least no one had been around to see it. Of that, he was certain. He'd left the Lasso at about 8:00 and took Bramble Road; the country lane never saw much traffic, let alone that late in the evening. And yeah, maybe he'd had a few too many with Reggie Hoyt, and maybe he wasn't "all there" at the wheel after that, but the fact still stood—no one hardly ever went down Bramble, so who would have expected some damn kid to . . . ?

Ray shook a bit as he recalled the thump and jostle his truck had made, and seemingly for no reason at all. He'd stopped immediately after that, the shock of the sound knocking away whatever buzz he'd still had; he didn't need to pull to the shoulder of the road, because he was already driving along it.

He'd got out, ran behind the bed—and saw the kid lying there. He hadn't spotted him until then—not a single solitary glimpse. The kid wasn't there, and then he just was. How couldn't he have seen him?

The kid might've been twenty-five; dark hair; deeply tanned; lying on a backpack strapped about his shoulders.

There was nothing Ray could have done for the guy. The kid was coughing up blood, for Christ's sake, and by the time Ray headed back to his truck, he had closed his eyes and gone still.

But the way he'd looked over at Ray just before that: eyes wide—afraid, questioning—and his cheek all torn up, blood sleeked along his face and over his shirt . . .

Ray put the bottle back up to his lips, but his hand shook as he tipped it back. The alcohol sneaked up into his nose and poured down his chin. He coughed and sputtered, pausing his pace as he wiped the back of his arm across the feverish skin of his jaw.

He gritted his teeth and forced his eyes shut, fighting that warm wetness that tingled across them. He *had* to get his shit together.

Hell, for all Ray knew, the kid was a damn illegal. Could've even been a fresh one; they were only thirty-odd miles from the border. Might've explained the backpack. But would anyone care about that, if the heat came down on Ray? Would anyone bother to think that the kid just *maybe* wasn't supposed to be here to begin with? Absolutely not. Some liberal bastards looking for blood would probably even say the whole mess was a hate crime and add a few extra years to Ray's sentence.

Weren't no hate to it, Ray thought, washing the idea down with another sip. *Just wrong place, wrong time. And I ain't about to go to prison for a—*

He turned back about, set to keep up his pacing—but something shocked him to a halt.

The kid he'd run over was sitting on his bed. But not his *actual* bed—he was sitting on the reflection of it in his closet mirror, right there on the corner, looking at Ray.

Ray looked from the empty space over his bed and back to the reflection, working the optical oddity over in his mind, but there wasn't a single answer to explain it.

The dead kid stared straight at him as he contemplated, looking as he had on that road: covered in blood, the skin of his face hanging in a raw flap, his backpack on, carrying things to help him through a life he wouldn't get to live.

And all because you killed me, the kid's cold, narrowed eyes seemed to say. *Killed me and left me for the coyotes, like I was some desert rodent.*

"There was nothing I could do," Ray mumbled, answering a voice that didn't exist. "I'm sorry, kid, but that's the cold, hard truth. Weren't any way to help. Now, just leave me be . . ."

But the kid just sat there, staring at him from his reflected death.

"You ain't real," Ray said, his tone gaining strength. "I'm just imagining you. Now, leave me be!"

The room seemed to be getting warmer. Sweat broke out along Ray's scalp and his head started to churn, like laundry in a spin cycle.

His lips had gone dry and his eyes were throbbing; he squeezed them, hoping the kid would be gone when he opened them again. But no such luck.

"Leave me be!" Ray groaned, his breaths growing ragged, his chest bobbing and tightening.

The kid kept staring, not saying a word. And he didn't have to, because Ray quickly broke under that awful gaze.

"*Leave me be*!"

As he shouted it, Ray wound his arm back and threw his beer bottle straight at the mirror. But his aim was off, way off, and rather than hitting the image of the dead youth, the bottle's bottom went smashing into the reflection of Ray's own chest, cracking the mirror in a spider-web's break. As the crack erupted across the glass, Ray felt a similar shattering through his own chest—his heart clenching under a swift and terrible pressure.

His breath seemed to leave him, along with the strength in his limbs. He was sinking to his knees, and then he was flat out on the floor.

Ray squirmed about like a worm on a hot sidewalk, looking up to his mirror and the image of the dead kid, who watched as he succumbed to the heart-attack.

Ray wanted to scream for help—but by that point, nothing could be done for him.

As he went still, the dead youth faded out of the mirror, leaving him there to the heat of the day.

Old Shuck

1825

"It's true enough, I tell you! I saw it myself, just the other night!"

"Bah!" Clarence Smith spat in return, waving off his friend's superstitious assertions. "No, you bloody did not."

"Yes, I did!" Gerald Jones maintained, following after Smith as they strode along the walkway. The din of three dozen running power looms rose up from below them, the constant whirling noise filling the entire cotton mill. Late afternoon light stole its way through the grime-coated windows about them, the dusty air stirring as though it were alive.

"You may very well have seen a black dog," Smith retorted, growing more and more exasperated with his friend, "but you didn't see no Old Shuck!"

"Yes, I did!" Jones repeated, pointing an accusatory finger to the other foreman's back. "I came out of my house the morning 'fore last, in the thick of all that rain we had, and as I made my less-than-merry way onto Silk Street, I looked down an alley, and there it was! A great big dog—the biggest damned hound I ever laid eyes upon—with a shaggy coat of fur that was coal-black. And its eyes were raging red, like the fires of Perdition itself! My ghost nearly left my bones then and there, I'll warrant! Then it was gone, back into the shadows."

Smith shook his head, gazing down at his feet with a smirk as they kept on around the walkway. Jones, however, was far from through.

"And I'm not the only one who's seen it, either! That infernal thing's been sighted all over Manchester these last weeks, and it's a certain omen of death to whoever comes upon it! Just the other day, some tradesman said he saw it before the cathedral, of all places! And that four-legged demon *leapt* upon him, snarling and barking! Not satisfied with letting him die in good time, it seems! And you know what else? The cathedral is only a short way off from where *I* saw the beast on Silk Street!"

"Oh, indeed?" Smith sighed, stopping and turning about to face his friend. "Well, maybe that tradesman had himself a good nip of the bottle that evening, and Old Shuck smelled it on him from all the way down in the underworld; crawled on up to ask the git for a taste of its own!"

Smith gave a chuckle, lifting his hands as a tired mother would before a fitful child. "As a matter of fact, I bet all of these superstitious clods who claim to be seeing devil-dogs about had a good nip or two before their *terrible* encounters! So tell me, Jonesy—and be honest—what did *you* have the morning of yours? A snifter of brandy or a full pint of lager?"

"Laugh now," Jones said, eyes wide and skin pale, "but let's see if you do the same after I'm dead within the month! Try and have a good giggle when you're attending my funeral, why don't you?"

"Oh, 'swounds! Would you—?"

"Gentlemen!"

The scratchy, albeit commanding voice rose up behind them. Its lashing notes were all too familiar to the men, and they stiffened rightly as they turned to face Alastair Harris, owner and overseer of the mill. He stood at their backs, his ashen face glowering, as per usual.

"I neither pay you to waste the day talking of supernatural drivel, nor to block my walkways and bar me from my office." His steely stare shifted between them. "Do I?"

"No, sir," Smith answered, his grin abashed.

"Absolutely not, sir," Jones agreed, his fervor effectively sobered under his employer's gaze.

Harris nodded with finality. "Then desist in both and get back to work."

Smith and Jones slipped aside, allowing their employer to pass between them.

Harris' feet smacked against the walkway as he continued on towards his office, which hung nestled in the dark corner of the mill, looming over all below. He strode with his hands clasped behind his back, peering down his nose to the looms and those who were operating them, a cursory look to ensure that all was running well. Pleased with the work that he saw, he set his sights before him once more and turned his mind to other matters.

As he stepped into the office, his clerk and assistant, Harold Wilkinson, gave him a flustered and forcefully cheery greeting. Harris gave a hushed harrumph in return, moving right on towards his own, much larger desk across the room. He sat himself down and set to reading and signing miscellaneous paperwork, analyzing reports of his mill's output, and stewing in a brooding silence that seemed to ill-befit one so wealthy and well-off as he.

Wilkinson, meanwhile, saw to his own humble tasks. He did not dare so much as breathe a breath that was louder than the dull hum of the looms coming from beyond the walls; he moved and worked with the softness of a mouse before a patient trap, maintaining the silence as best as he could.

The staggering stillness was finally broken a quarter hour later, when shouting voices and rushed, clanging footsteps upon the walkways reached their ears.

The office door flung open, with one Samuel Taylor doing the flinging.

The recently sacked worker stood there with a solemn look on his bearded face, his clothes dirtied and the flat cap upon his head bearing a ratty hole.

One of the mill's portly guards came running up behind him, huffing a good deal.

"I'm sorry, sir!" the guard said to Harris, who remained behind his desk, looking at the scene with a calm demeanor; Wilkinson had risen to his feet, surprised at the outburst and ever fidgety. "I tried to stop 'im, but 'e ran right on past me at the post! Quite insistent, 'e seems!"

"Yes, I can see that," Harris said flatly. He set his pen and papers aside and clasped his hands, setting them on his desk, appearing attentive. "Gather your breath, now; you'll need it to see him out in a moment. In the meantime, would you care to explain this intrusion, Mr. Taylor? I seem to recall having released you from the mill not four days ago."

Taylor's sad face fell all the more as he spoke. "Yes, sir; I know, sir. But, please . . . I've come to ask you to reconsider. I need this job. Work is hard to find these days, after all. And I've worked your mill these last two years! Why, I know this place as well as I know my own body! I've given you good work!"

Harris made no motion, nor did his stony visage show the least measure of sympathy as he responded.

"Indeed, you did, Mr. Taylor. And "did" will remain the optimal word on the matter. You must understand that I—and many others in the business of textiles—appreciate the value of cheap labor. And I and other factory owners are coming to realize the cheapest labor comes from employing younger, spryer souls than you. A child can complete the tasks that you do here, and so one shall. Simple, efficient business, Mr. Taylor."

"But, sir," Taylor implored, stepping closer to Harris and his desk, "I have a family to take care of and to feed! They depend upon me and the wages I earn. Matters were difficult enough for us as they were; when I wasn't tending to the looms, I was out of the city, hunting just to put meat on the table! Why, without your employment—"

"You'll have plenty more time to spend in the woods, looking for more meat," Harris cut him off, growing tired of this matter now that he'd had his say. "I wish you luck in the hunt for both game and employment elsewhere."

The guard made to grab Taylor's arm, but Taylor shook it off. His face went from sorrowfully slack to angrily taut; his meek and mild begging became exasperated sighs.

"Sir, I *must* have my job back! I'm desperate. I have children, for God's sake! A boy and a girl, hungry and wanting in a cold home!"

Harris still did not seem moved in the least by the man's pleas. He blinked once, twice, and then spoke in that persisting, maddeningly blunt fashion.

"You are not the first "desperate" man that I have sacked, Mr. Taylor, and you certainly will not be the last. And while I do not receive any pleasure at terminating your employment, it will not set my heart to breaking, either. So, save your woes and your pleas for the unemployment line; they will win you naught here. As for your children: perhaps one of them may qualify for your old job. I suggest you bring the boy in, if you are in such dire straits; we pay the boys a halfpenny more."

Silence settled over the room for a prolonged moment as Samuel Taylor glared at Harris, enraged tears at the corners of his eyes. The tears were the only remaining hint of his sorrow; the rest of him—from his shaking frame to his fiery-red face—spoke of the rage that had taken him as he listened to his former employer's callous words.

"There's a special place in hell for people like you, Harris," Taylor sneered. "People who use and play with their fellow man, like a dog with a bone."

Harris' stone face finally broke at this insult—and it broke into a small, careless smile. "And I'm sure there's a special place in your Heaven for those who live and die poor." He lifted a hand, motioning to the guard. "Please see Mr. Taylor out now."

The guard grabbed Taylor's elbow again, and this time, Taylor allowed it. He side-stepped along as he was rushed out, and before the guard shut the door behind them, Taylor glared back at Harris and said: "You'll pay for this, you bastard."

"Perhaps," Harris said to the musty air a moment later, "but then, *I* can afford to."

He returned to his papers, going on with his duties as though nothing had interrupted him, let alone vexed him. Wilkinson, who had watched the whole ordeal in mute dismay, sat back down and tried to continue on with his work, in kind, a perturbing knot in his gut. It gave a twist when Harris spoke to him.

"You will have to stay late this evening, Wilkinson. I will need your help in going over and completing textile orders."

"Y— yes, sir, Mr. Harris," Wilkinson stammered.

The clerk went back to his papers, lamenting that he would have to spend an extra hour or two with the ever-demanding, ever-unfeeling Alastair Harris.

And so the hours crept by until the mill closed, its workers shambling homewards as the western sky shined with the last lingering glow of sunset. Harris, Wilkinson, and the lone, portly guard were the only ones left in the factory by the time night had settled in full. It wasn't until the clock was on the verge of striking nine that the three stepped out into the streets, their day finally at an end.

The men bundled up against the slight chill of the evening, the guard and Wilkinson giving Harris their insincere farewells. Harris gave them a half-hearted wave of his hand, turning his back on them as each made their way down a different street and homewards.

The sporadic lampposts here and about had been lit and now shone overhead, casting the streets into increments of golden light and cowering shadow, where the light could not fully reach. The sky above was veiled in soupy clouds, the promise of a full moon's glow shining only dimly through and beyond the buildup; there were no stars to speak of in the heavens, nor souls to see across the earth. The streets were quite barren at this hour. Harris' leisurely steps plodded against the cobblestone and through the stillness, echoing off of the gray faces of the looming buildings about him.

He walked on for a few dim blocks, unperturbed and lost to thoughts of business, before the distant knell of the striking hour rang out through the night.

No sooner had their song started then he heard the sound of animalistic growling coming from somewhere in the shadows about him.

Harris slowed to a halt, the noise awakening some caution in him. He gazed ahead and then back the way he had come, seeing no sign of any creature along the street. He listened for the patter of feet, the swish of a tail, or another troubled growl, but all had gone still yet again.

He began to think that he had heard nothing at all, save for some silly whit of his imagination.

Satisfied enough with this, he made to continue on; but before he could even lift his foot for another assured step, the sound of some hound giving a rough clearing of its nose staid him.

He turned about, looking nervously to the other side of the street, where the great doorway of an office building sat shrouded in the night.

In that moment, the machinations of the universe (or perhaps some darker, smirking force) came into perfect, terrible alignment: as another tolling of the bell sounded out, and as the low growling picked up once more, the clouds overhead began to shift. They slipped from each other—like woven fingers unweaving—just enough to send a shaft of moonlight shooting to the earth, falling upon the threshold of that blackened doorway that held Harris' eye. And in that gradual illumination, he saw the dark form of a great big dog, sitting at attention and looking straight at him.

Harris observed the beast and its menacing presence with a dawning sense of foreboding.

Its obsidian fur held the shimmer of the light, growing thick and wild about its bulk of a body. Its legs and its haunches looked astonishingly muscular and long, and its head was equally large, ears pointed up and poised like a statue. Dagger-edged teeth poked out of its long maw, its lips turned up in its continuing snarl.

But the most sinister of all its mighty canine attributes, by far, were its eyes. They were narrowed, and they shined with an unnatural scarlet essence, as though fashioned from the very first torrid fires that Hell had ever known. It was quite an impossible thing, and yet there they were, their terrible sights upon Harris—and it chilled his very spirit to know it.

He recalled the argument he'd heard just that afternoon, stuck behind the bantering Clarence Smith and the high-strung Gerald Jones; he remembered his burning irritation and near nausea at hearing talk of "devil-dogs" and the foolish like. But now, with this unholy thing before his very eyes, he was forced to reckon such blatant disregard of otherworldly things. His rational mind was all of a sudden dashed upon the stones of doubt, and he feared that his skin—indeed, his very soul—could now be rent by the teeth of this bizarre creature.

That dread went soaring to new heights as the hound raised its head towards the moon and let loose a call that was caught between a wolf's howl and a phantom's wail.

This awful sound was what finally loosened Harris' knees and set his feet to racing down the street.

He ran faster than he ever had before, caught in a maelstrom of fear. His soles smacked along the cobblestones and his coat billowed out as he made to dash down a side alley. The dark and narrow way became filled with the racket of his steps, his whimpering, and yet another howl from the creature, the baying rising and falling over him like a sea's wave. It pushed him on and out into the next street, then on to the next, and he kept on running until the howling trailed off to silence.

Harris paused, just long enough to listen to the alleys. His ears discerned the scratching of nails upon stones and the ragged breaths of the beast at his back. It was chasing after him.

Harris dashed off again, taking alleyways and streets as they came, not rightly thinking of where he was going; the only thought in his head was the desperate hope of some sanctuary. He cried out as he went, eyes locked ahead, imploring someone to help and shelter him, and begging a God he had never put faith in to save his soul. But the streets remained desolate, all the doors stayed shut, and nary an angel swooped down to lift him on high.

The calamitous noise of growling and the persistent patter of paws filled the night, as though all the hounds of Hell were now racing after him. It was driving him to the edge of his sanity, and eventually, to the edge of the River Irwell.

Heaving his labored breaths, he kept on along a paved path beside the narrow portion of the stretching waterway. A small stone bridge hung just overhead, arching over to the next bank and casting the path into a length of shadow.

As he entered that darkness, Harris' weary legs finally failed him. He gave a cry as he tumbled face-first onto the cold stones. All of his breath left him as his chest hit the ground, his sides erupting with instant pain. The yapping and snarling grew nearer as he struggled to crawl on, tears in his eyes and pleas at his quivering lips. When he felt teeth digging into his calf and dragging him back, his entreaties gave way to his screams.

He heard his trousers rip and felt flesh and muscle tearing away from his leg. As he dug his fingers into the ground—and to his ever-growing surprise—another pair of jaws came gnashing into his wrist; the black devil-dog was not alone.

Harris looked to his bloodied, agony-stricken arm and saw that it was a black and brown German Shepherd that had a hold of his wrist, a collar about its leashed neck; looking back, he saw a Doberman Pinscher—likewise leashed—still tearing at his heel. And worse yet, another one came running up to join its compatriots in the slaughter.

The devil-dog, it turned out, was nowhere in sight. That fact provided him little solace as the three canines unleashed their fury upon him as one, biting and rending his limbs as they sleeked their tongues with his blood. His wails rose all the more as he tried to break free, to no avail.

Those mournful cries had reached Samuel Taylor's ears long before he caught up with his hunting dogs and their grisly kill. The slighted man slowed his run as soon as the bridge came into sight, and he approached the shadowed underpass with gradual, uncertain steps.

This was what he had wanted; this was how he would see his threat to Harris fulfilled.

After Harris' insult, he had returned home, rallying up and leading his hunting dogs through the night for this purpose alone. He had no intention of simply scaring his former employer with their presence; Harris' cold words had seen to that, sending the chill of bloody vengeance into his heart, instead. He had sat with them for hours in the shadow of the mill, just waiting for Harris to leave. When he had, Taylor pushed the dogs on, tracking the businessman through the streets until the opportune moment arose—when Taylor felt he could loose them upon the bastard and let them have their way with him.

"I wish you luck in the hunt." Taylor had laughed at Harris' own words, for luck was just what they'd had in slinking quietly through the streets, keeping their presence at his back unknown. They had fallen no more than a block behind him all the while. However, after some other dog's wild howl had risen up through the streets, his own dogs' orneriness could not be contained any longer. At that moment, they had pulled against their leashes with such force that they slipped from Taylor's grip. They went on after Harris of their own accord, snarling and bolting off like rabid beasts with the scent of blood. Taylor chased after them as they chased down Harris, and now, here they all were.

His revenge upon his former employer had come to pass; but as much as he had yearned for it, to see it meted out . . .

It was far more terrible than he could have imagined. He watched the silhouettes of his dogs pulling apart the shadow that was Alastair Harris with a mixture of both vindication and revulsion.

The *sounds* . . .

That *screaming* . . .

His stomach gave a lurch as Harris' yells started to grow weak and ragged. He turned away from the scene, his whole body caught between rage and disgust and shaking with their conflict. He looked to the river for a moment, and then back down the path trailing beside it.

He froze as he caught sight of a great black dog sitting alert in the middle of the path. Its eyes of burning red stared at him through the darkness.

He kept his eyes fast upon it, until Harris' grunts had turned to whimpers, and then stopped altogether. His dog's came stepping up to him a moment later, their noses wet and red and leashes scraping the ground. They sat at his side, bowing their heads and whining lightly as they, too, noticed the curiously large hound.

A moment crept by as Taylor and the beast continued observing one another. Then, the dog rose, turned about, and returned to wherever it had come from, dashing off into the night.

Swallowing down the lump in his throat, Taylor snatched up his dogs' leashes. He led them over to the river's edge, where he knelt and cupped his hands in the water, pouring it onto the snout of each dog, washing away the blood. After the quick cleaning, he rushed them along and homewards. He refused to look back at the shadow-covered scraps of what was once Alastair Harris.

***

Harris' body would be discovered the following day, its terrible state sparking further rumors and fears of Old Shuck making its rounds about the city, dispensing death in the wake of its appearance.

A week later, Samuel Taylor died quite unexpectedly, having been trampled after a team of spooked horses brought their hooves and their carriage bearing down upon him in the streets. None who witnessed the tragedy could explain what had terrified and stirred the horses into such action.

Another week later, the superstitious Gerald Jones succumbed to a sudden and nasty affliction of the flu that had brought him low days before. His friend, Clarence Smith, did not laugh in the least when attending his funeral.

Damned Happy

It was Amy Higgins' fifth birthday. The little girl was gleefully waiting for her party to begin. In another hour, she'd be surrounded by ten of her closest friends (all girls, of course; no stinky boys could be allowed into such an exclusive event), delicious cake, wrapped presents, and in the spotlight of attention.

Meanwhile, her father, James, was on the verge of slipping into hysterics.

Because in another hour, the clown would arrive.

***

It was a sunny and pleasant June day—the perfect time for a birthday party in the backyard of the Higgins' home.

Amy sat at the head of a picnic table on the lawn, her friends clustered about her. For the last ten minutes, they'd been shoveling in the birthday cake with relish. White and pink icing and specs of chocolate cake covered the corners of their wide smiles. When they weren't focused on the tasty cake, they laughed and talked, squealing in a child's joy. They pointed and giggled at the characters on the Sofia the First table-spread under their plates. Amy kept prying for hints as to what were in the wrapped boxes and decorated bags sitting on a separate table a few feet from them; each of her friends would shake their head and laugh, saying "I won't tell!" and "You'll just have to see!"

Sitting above them, up on the wooden deck of the Higgins' home, were their parents. In between chatting about more grown-up topics like healthcare and gas prices, they would watch their kids, laughing at their innocent fun and joy.

Except for James Higgins.

He tried. He really did. He tried to take pleasure in his daughter's big day—*knew* that he should—but he just couldn't.

He kept thinking about the clown, and he knew it would be showing up at any moment.

He sat quietly, hunkered in between his wife, Karen, and their next-door neighbor, Jim Scofield. Every now and then, he shot Karen a dirty look, one she never saw but that he enjoyed showing nevertheless. He knew it wasn't fair to do so; she wasn't really to blame. She didn't know about his fear, because he hadn't told her about it.

He fought against hiring a clown for Amy's party, but had ultimately lost. He came up with every manner of excuse possible to dissuade his wife from calling the number on the advertisement for a performing local clown she'd found in the newspaper. But Karen was resolute, and Amy was thrilled when they'd told her about the performer coming to her party.

Maybe if he had tried to make them understand his deep-seeded dislike of clowns, he could have made them change their minds. Maybe they would see what clowns were actually like—how he saw them for what they truly were. But even he wasn't sure where his fear of their goofy, weird ilk came from, so how could he explain it to his family?

He'd never once been to a carnival or a circus in his life, and had never even met a clown up close. And it wasn't Stephen King's *It* that had spawned a life-long fear when he had watched it in his youth, though he still didn't care for it to this day.

No, his fear was somehow inherent, a primeval sense of knowing that clowns, their appearance, and their antics were simply not right. It was a knowledge he'd had since birth.

Clowns were just plain unnatural to him. "They're like the demon-seed of Jim Carrey and an Avon Lady from hell," an old college buddy had once joked. To James, that was an understatement. Their pale, white make-up made them look like the dead to him: like walking, talking corpses of long dead people who had been made to dress silly to hide their true, twisted nature beneath. And they always seemed so happy—always smiling and joking and jumping about. Nothing and nobody was meant to be that damned happy all the time, or so James had always thought.

The squeak of a bike horn rose above the murmur of the grown-ups' chatter and the children's laughter. It was followed by a quick succession of squeaks and exaggerated, giddy chuckling.

James spun his head around, searching for the source of the horn and the chuckling. It was coming from the other side of the backyard's wooden fence, near the door that led from the backyard and out to the street. James' stomach grew cold as he saw a collection of bright, multicolored balloons floating up above the fence's panels, bobbing lightly in the afternoon breeze, looking to James like a stalking cobra waiting to strike.

As all eyes turned to the fence, the door swung open. The balloons snuck their way through the entrance, and following them, the clown.

James clutched at the arms of his chair as the thing entered the backyard. It was as bad as he imagined it would be, if not even worse.

Puffy red and white pinstriped pants covered its legs, the cuffs flared out and hoop-like. Below the cuff line were the typical giant red shoes, protruding outwards. Canary yellow suspenders held the absurd pants up, stretching over a slim upper body clothed in a deep purple shirt with pink frills attached at the neckline and arm cuffs. A scarlet bow of obnoxious size sat at its neck, like a big red butterfly had nestled on its chest. Curly orange hair hung down to chin level around a stark white face, save for black-painted lips and a yellow sun and its sunbeams covering the clown's left eye. Finishing the purposefully goofy attire was a stubby black top-hat perched on the clown's head and set at a playful angle. The balloons, bobbing on their strings, were held in his right hand as he pulled a red wagon behind him. There was a cluster of props and items in it.

James watched as that pale face rose into a gleeful stare and those black lips parted ever-wider to form those loud guffaws.

Sweat broke out on James' forehead as the clown finally spoke.

"Hey, all! Yuck-Yuck the Clown is here to make your smiles wider! Yuck-yuck!"

The clown's words mingled with its sporadic chuckles. The children, their attention instantaneously switched from cake and ice-cream to the new arrival, began giggling and clapping. Amy lifted her hands up and out in greeting to the clown, waving them in pure excitement. Yuck-Yuck saw her, let go of the wagon, and waved at her in return, his smile growing even larger.

James felt a pang cut through his chest as the clown moved closer to his daughter.

Yuck-Yuck, bringing his chuckles to a more reserved level, stepped up to the table where the kids sat. He made his strides long and awkwardly lanky, which the children giggled at. He began passing out his collection of balloons to each of them, patting them on the head as he gave them the color of their choice.

James felt the urge to rush down the deck when the clown's hand ruffled Amy's hair, felt like he should charge in to fight off the strange creature that was trying to trick his daughter, to be the hero that saved the day from the wily, macabre thing. Instead, he reasoned with himself. Such actions would scare the children, upset the parents, and cause a scene.

Besides, if he were to save his daughter, he'd have to get close to the clown. Avoiding that was reason enough to keep his seat.

While he had been temporarily lost in thought, Yuck-Yuck had begun his little performance. James focused in on it now, watching the clown's every move in rigid attentiveness.

"Well, I know you kids like balloons, but do you like animals?" the clown was asking.

A cheer rose up from the children's table.

Yuck-Yuck turned his back to both the kids and the parents, reaching into one of the pockets of his pants and hunkering himself down to where no one could see what he was doing. He began doing a silly dance, shaking his behind in a way that James found to be rather obscene. Yuck-Yuck sprang up and around a few seconds later, a dog-shaped balloon animal held in his hands. The clown's laughter shifted into short, raspy barks as he mimicked the balloon-dog running about in the air. His impersonation was spot-on, sounding like a tiny, upset Chihuahua. The exactness was too spot-on for James, and he found it eerie.

Setting the balloon animal on the ground, Yuck-Yuck moved to his wagon. He reached in and pulled out a toy car that looked like a clown car, colored red and white. Across the windows were stenciled designs of clowns bunched up and clustered together within, some looking jovial while others looked irritated, pressing against each other and against the windows in a confined bunch. Yuck-Yuck turned a key built into the side of the car, winding it up and letting it go. A circus ditty began playing from somewhere in the car, surprisingly loud for so small a toy.

Yuck-Yuck held the car out to Amy.

"For the birthday girl," he chuckled out.

Amy accepted it with glee, squealing as she looked it over and as her friends clustered around her to see the gift. Turning his attention from the kids to the grown-ups on the deck, Yuck-Yuck continued.

"A little something to *drive* your parents wild!"

James swallowed down hard. He would have sworn the clown was looking directly at him when he said the horrible pun, and that the clown's constant smile wavered briefly into something of a snarl.

Then the clown turned his attention back to the children; James sunk further into his deck-chair, all the same, making himself small.

"Hey, kiddos, who here loves . . . magic?"

The kids all began raising their hands, their eyes widening.

Yuck-Yuck nodded and put his hand to his chin, rubbing it as if in deep thought.

"Gee," he said, "I think I need a volunteer to help with my next bit . . ."

The children's hands shot up as they waved back and forth in a frenzy for attention. Yuck-Yuck looked each over slowly before turning to face the parents on the deck. Yuck-Yuck's eyes fell on James and stayed there, the yellow sun over the clown's one eye scrunching as his sights narrowed.

"I think that Gloomy Gus there would be the perfect helper!"

The kids and the parents turned their attention to James as Yuck-Yuck pointed directly at him. The children sighed in disappointment, except for Amy, who clapped, giggled, and started chanting: "Yay, Daddy!"

James looked from Karen to the other parents around him, like a drowning man keeping his head above the wake, hoping for someone to notice him. Karen gave him an apologetic shrug, forcing a smile in spite of her husband's obvious dissatisfaction. The other grown-ups, however, laughed, glad to not have been chosen by the clown themselves and saying mocking words of encouragement to James.

James raised a hand up to ward off the attention and shook his head, eyes once again on the clown. That cold sensation in his stomach dropped another few degrees as he realized the clown was already up the steps of the deck and approaching the table.

Yuck-Yuck stopped right beside James, the clown leaning over him and staring down at him with a stare that had James riveted to his seat. Up close, James could see how the clown's white make-up was cracking, minuscule fissures in the sheen of the white looking to James like the veins of a pale, dead corpse going bad. The bright colors of the clown's outfit made James' eyes water, his growing fear adding some moisture to the corners of his eyes, as well. The clown's mocking laughter pounded in James' eardrums, so loud that he could barely hear the moan of worry that escaped his own throat. He had no choice but to stare into Yuck-Yuck's wide, overtly cheerful eyes as the clown bore down on him.

Yuck-Yuck lifted a hand to the kids, showing both the front and back sides. Then he showed it to the parents, making sure they realized nothing was in his hand. Then Yuck-Yuck whirled back on James, putting his painted face up to his own and sticking his hand right under James' nose.

"Can you spare some change, sir?" Yuck-Yuck asked, grinning wide. His teeth were a yellowish-white, and a strange, unrecognizable odor wafted on his breath that made James even sicker to his stomach.

James shook his head violently, hoping that the clown would just go away. But it wouldn't.

"Oh, I think you can!" Yuck-Yuck declared. He moved his hand up and began to close in on James, the clown's fingers clawing at the side of James' head.

That was what forced James to finally move, to break from his paralysis and do something, anything, to save himself.

He lifted his hands up and swatted the clown's hand away, rising up out of his deck-chair in a rush. He scanned the puzzled faces of his wife, his daughter, his neighbors, and the kids, each looking dismayed at him. Yuck-Yuck stood still, smiling a knowing smile.

James stammered over his words as he backed away from the clown and towards the backdoor of the house.

"I . . . I, uh . . . I'm just not feeling very well." James turned his back on the clown and the others and rushed to the door. "I think . . . I'm going to be sick."

Without a word from the others, James rushed into the house, feeling instantly more secure. He walked into the kitchen and stopped by the sink looking out to the deck and to the backyard. He brushed away the sweat on his forehead and peered outside, wondering what was going on now.

Yuck-Yuck had walked off the deck and was back in the yard, pulling out a horn and an umbrella for some other part of his act. Karen, Amy, and the others were all focused on him again, James' odd behavior forgotten and the spirit of the party back in full swing.

James watched from the kitchen window with tense muscles and a gaze that never left the clown and its antics. He waited and watched the clown to see if it made anymore strange or questionable moves towards his wife or his daughter, watched and waited for it to break from its cheerful facade to reveal the nasty, odd thing that James knew it to truly be.

But he didn't go back outside until the clown had left, and never once thought to until it had.

***

The Higgins had decided to call it an early night. Amy, tuckered out from her party, and from opening her presents and then playing with them all for hours, was now deep in sleep in her bedroom. Karen slept peacefully next to James, weary from the clean-up of the party and watching after the children as they'd played in the backyard.

James lay in bed, wide awake, reflecting on the day and his fears.

As soon as Yuck-Yuck had been paid and left the party, James left his watch at the kitchen sink and came back out. He claimed he had gotten sick, a combination of too much cake and the heat of the day. He hadn't eaten more than a single piece of birthday cake and the day had been a moderate 70 degrees, but Karen seemed to accept his excuse, saying she'd seen how he was sweating and shaking and how he looked just terrible. If only she knew the half of it.

James was tempted to come out and admit his trepidation towards clowns, to explain to his wife why he had acted the way he did. He needed to try and justify it, both for himself and to Karen. But he just couldn't. As he formulated a reasonable explanation of his fear, the smell on Yuck-Yuck's breath came back to him in force, and the smile that the clown had shown as he retreated in cowardice filled his thoughts.

James couldn't bear the thought of falling asleep only to dream of the clown from his daughter's party, its absurd appearance made all the worse through the contortions and molding of a horrific nightmare. Instead of holding colorful balloons, the clown would have his friends' and neighbors' heads floating above it, strings in hand. It would stand a hundred feet tall, leaning down to prey upon him, breathing on him with that horrible breath, now reeking of blood and flesh and filth. It would honk its horn incessantly, but instead of playful squeaks, each squeeze would sound out screams—screams that sounded like his wife and daughter. Then, the clown would squash him with its enormous red shoe . . .

The clamor of a car alarm going off made James jump and brought him out of his grim thoughts.

The horn blared from somewhere not far off, and it was incredibly loud. Karen stirred a little beside him, but she didn't wake. James laughed lightly as he felt his heart easing its quickened beat. He had worked himself up into a fit with his contemplation of the clown, and the shock of the car horn had jogged him out of what he now saw as fruitless worrying.

He waited for the car horn to stop bleating, for silence to come back. And he waited. And he waited. But the horn would not stop.

Growing irritated, James sat up in bed. Karen was stirring more and more, letting out a light groan of disapproval as the alarm kept going. Sighing, James swung his legs out of the bed and put on his slippers. If he couldn't stop the car alarm, at least he could go downstairs, take a look out the window, and see whose car was making the racket so he could thoroughly cuss them out tomorrow morning.

James left their bedroom and made his way down the hall. He stopped at Amy's bedroom, cracking the door open slowly and quietly, checking to see if his little girl was awakened by the noise. She was snoring lightly, curled up in her Dora the Explorer bed sheets.

James shut the door and moved on. The things kids could sleep through.

He made his way down the stairs. Each step he descended brought him closer to the noise of the honking car, and as he walked towards the living room, it hit James: the noise was *extremely* close.

And it wasn't coming from outside.

Stopping in the doorway of the living room, James looked around, scanning. The noise was definitely coming from within the room—inexplicably so, but it was. It was reaching a fever pitch, making his ears ache and his temples throb.

His discomfort was forgotten the moment he saw where the noise was coming from.

It was coming from Amy's toy car sitting on the floor. The one Yuck-Yuck the Clown had given her at the party.

The tiny plastic thing was rocking side to side, as if something were having a fit within it. The headlights in its front were flashing, sending thin beams of yellow light across the room. The honking horn kept beating away as the car jolted and jived.

Until it just stopped.

James stood there, unsure of whether or not he'd really just seen what he thought he had seen. Before he had much time to think, though, the car's music started playing its circus theme, and something popped out of the car, jutting from the toy's driver side. Straining his eyes in the dark of the night, James could just barely tell what it was.

A finger. A human-sized finger, painted white.

Then the finger became a human-sized hand, squeezing its impossible way out. A human-sized arm followed the hand, clad in a familiar purple shirt sleeve with pink frills at the cuff. Then a human sized-head poked out of the minuscule window, swelling out like the inflation of a balloon, the silhouette of a pudgy top-hat on top and chin-length hair hanging around it. The head was grinning maniacally.

It was Yuck-Yuck the Clown.

James felt every muscle in his body tighten as the rest of the clown popped out of the car, its entire body somehow shooting out of the toy car's window. The clown tumbled onto the floor with a thud. Then, leaping up to its large red feet, the clown giggled and held its arms out in welcome, the sheen of its yellow-white smile aimed at James.

"Woulda' got here sooner, bud," the clown practically shouted in between its chuckles, "but car-pooling can be a real bitch, you know what I mean?"

James blinked hard, praying he was dreaming, or maybe just outright losing his mind—anything that would mean that the clown before him wasn't really there.

But it was. And it was happy to see him.

"I came back to finish my act!" the clown proclaimed. It hitched up its pants, mimicking getting ready for some hard labor. Then it started making its way towards James, slamming its feet down with each step.

James' mind could only register a single thought: run.

And run he did. He found himself turning, heading back to the stairs. The thought of protecting his wife and child from the otherworldly clown came to mind; but as he heard a mocking snort from behind him, he knew that the clown had come for him, and him alone. The realization made him only want to move faster.

James took the steps two at a time, nearly tripping halfway up. He caught himself, though, pushing back up and managing to reach the top. He spared a glance towards the clown, seeing how close it was in its pursuit.

It stood at the foot of the stairs, arms crossed over its chest, laughing and smiling sinisterly.

"Going up!" it squealed.

It hopped onto the first step, lifted a leg over the banister, and set itself down, its back towards James. Then, as it giggled, it began sliding up the banister, defying all laws of gravity, gliding backwards up the stairs. It reached the top in a split second. It looked around at James, amused at his apparent shock.

"Second floor, Wussy Department!" the clown said, lifting its leg back over the banister to continue the chase.

James groaned and turned around, aiming to head for his and Karen's bedroom; but the hallway had changed, and drastically so.

The hall was no longer that of his home's, but that of some carnival funhouse attraction. The short hall was now yards and yards long, the door to his and Karen's bedroom a dark speck at its far end. The walls were no longer a dark blue; they were a deep red, made even redder by circular light fixtures set into the ceiling that had not been there before, giving off a dim pinkish light that lit the macabre hall. And all the way down to the end, and on both sides, the walls were lined with body-length funhouse mirrors.

Hearing the clown's laughter getting closer and hearing the rustling of its ridiculous clothing behind him, James hauled ass. He'd save understanding for later; now was the time to flee.

Pumping his arms and thrusting his legs with all his might, he began to clear the distance of the hall. As he passed by each mirror, he noticed out of the corner of his eye that the images reflected in each changed from one mirror to the next. Each reflection was of him in his matching light blue pajama top and bottoms, but he himself was different in every reflection. He saw a rail-thin, skinny version of himself; an enormously fat one; a minuscule one with tiny arms and legs; a freakishly tall version with tree-stump legs; and numerous ones in which he was of a different ethnicity. He even noticed a reflection on his right that showed him as a rather busty blonde woman that barely fit into his pajamas.

But the worst of them, by far, was of him as nothing but a skeleton, a pile of scurrying bones rattling as they ran.

It eventually felt like he'd been running for minutes, yet when he looked down at the bedroom door at the end of the hall, it was the same distance away as when he'd started running. He hadn't seemed to have gotten any closer.

James' muscles began to ache with exhaustion. And he was starting to lose his breath.

He hazarded a glance back at the clown.

Yuck-Yuck was standing where he'd left him, bent over with hands on his pin-striped knees, slapping them in laughter as he watched James run. The clown started running around in a circle when he saw James look back, ridiculing his efforts to escape. The clown stopped after a few more round-abouts and pointed down to James.

"Hey!" the clown called out. "Is this a hammer in my pocket, or am I just happy to see you?"

The clown planted its feet and set its hands to the zipper of its pants. With a quick downward thrust, the flap of its pants was undone and open. The clown placed its hands on its hips and laughed.

"Why, I think it's both!"

Then something shot out of the hole in the pants, extending out as it careened down the hall and closed in on James. It glinted in the pink light of the hall as it neared.

James realized it was a sledge-hammer, its wooden shaft extending out from the clown's crotch as its large silver head shot down towards him.

The head of the hammer struck James' lower back with great force. Pain swept over James' back as he tumbled forward from the blow.

Somehow, as he was pushed forward by the force of the hammer, James' flailing body cleared the distance to the far-off bedroom door; he crashed right through the wooden frame, sending the door into splinters and chunks.

He landed with a thud on a dirt floor, his face planted into rough grains of earth. A roar of clapping hands erupted around him as he slowly made his way up, his body racked with pain. He stood on shaking legs as he saw that his bedroom, like the hallway, had radically changed.

The smells of cotton-candy and decay mingled in the air.

His and Karen's bed lay in the middle of a great big circus tent, right under the big-top, the only other sign of their old room being the nightstand on James' side of the bed. Orange and yellow-striped walls of cloth rose up around him, stretching up to the spiraled point of the tent's concave top.

Around the circular edge of the tent were rows of wooden benches. To James' dismay, he realized they were all filled.

A horde of clowns sat on the benches, of all colors and sizes, done up in their silly wardrobe and their face-paints, grinning as they watched James. Their smiles spoke of mirth, but their narrowed eyes screamed hatred and condemnation upon James, and he cowered under their sights. Sprinkled throughout the crowd were dead, long decayed bodies, with loose, gray and blue skin that hung from white bones. They sat hunched over, heads tilted awkwardly but in a way that each could lay their eyes (or eye-sockets) on James

It was these on-looking clowns and corpses that were clapping so vehemently. And all for James.

James looked towards his and Karen's bed. The sheets had been pulled all the way up and over, and the only thing he could see of his wife was the curves of her form beneath the covers. He moaned as he moved forward, both from the ache of his battered body and at the thought of what he'd find under the covers.

He hobbled forward. He paid no attention to the crowd that watched him, although his stomach turned under their gaze. He stepped up to the bed, grabbed the covers, and thrust them away.

His wife turned into a bobo doll the instant he removed the sheets. Her body shifted from its normal self into the stout, round, plastic blow-up doll within the tick of a second. The stenciled design on its front was a caricature of Karen, an exaggerated cartoon of herself, including her nightgown, her hair, and her peaceful, sleeping face. James would have screamed at this, if he were capable—but all voice of protest had lodged in his aching throat as he took in what his wife had become.

He jumped and fell into the bed as Yuck-Yuck appeared directly behind him, thrusting its face up to his.

"N— No!" James shouted, pushing himself up against the headboard. There was nowhere left to run, nowhere to escape to.

The clown bore down on him, forcing him to lay flat against the bed as Yuck-Yuck hovered over him.

The clown was laughing louder now, its teeth bared in its victory and trickery. Each tooth was now an elongated fang and discolored by gray and yellow splotches. They glinted in the light of the tent as the clown spoke.

"I told ya', I'm here to finish my act!"

Spittle flew as the clown let out one huge guffaw and reached a hand towards James' head.

Its fingers clawed at the side of his face, and James could do nothing but wait for it to tear at his flesh, to crush his skull, to snap his neck . . .

To pull a coin from behind his ear, as Yuck-Yuck inexplicably did.

One instant the clown looked enraged and bloodthirsty, but as it pulled its hand back, a shiny silver dollar between its thumb and forefinger, it smiled in sheer joy. It waved the other hand in front of the coin, showing off his trick to James.

"See," it giggled, "I knew you could spare some change!"

James didn't know how to react. He stayed silent, body still rigid, waiting for death, but the clown eased away from him. It lost the glimmer of menace in its eyes as it looked over the coin. The clapping of the crowd trickled down until silence filled the big-top.

Yuck-Yuck turned his sights to James and then back to the coin. His smile lowered until it was a mere smirk of bitter pleasure.

"Tell you what," the clown said, its jovial voice gone and replaced by a deep, gravelly tone. "I'll let you keep this. As a reminder . . ."

It leaned in towards James. When Yuck-Yuck spoke, it was in his original voice, goofy and riddled with cheer.

"Remember, bud: it's those fucking mimes that'll kill ya'!"

Yuck-Yuck stepped back, lifted its arm with coin in hand, and brought it slamming down onto the nightstand.

And then everything was back to normal.

The tent was gone, the big-top was gone, and the crowd was gone. Most importantly, Yuck-Yuck was gone.

James raised himself up, looking over the dark bedroom with wide, disbelieving eyes. The room was returned to its usual state. The door had not been shattered or broken. Karen slept noiselessly beside him, beautiful flesh and bone once more.

He had to make sure it was real, though. James shook Karen, grabbing her shoulder and calling her name loudly. She woke up with a start and a puzzled look on her face.

"James . . . James, what's going on? Are you okay?"

Her voice filled him with joy and he nodded his head in elation. Laughing, practically giddy, he wrapped his arms around her, holding her. She accepted it, though hesitantly, and patted his back, like a mother comforting a child after a nightmare.

"I'm fine, sweetheart. I'm fine, I'm fine, I'm fine! Thank God!"

He couldn't hold back his laughter, and he let it flow out from him. It faltered the instant he remembered, though. He whirled around and looked at the nightstand.

There on the table-top was a shining silver dollar.

James felt the fear surge through him. Realization dawned that all he had just experienced was no nightmare, no night terror, not even a bout of insanity—it was real. But despite this, he continued to laugh.

Karen put a loving hand on his cheek, pulling him back to her. She looked worried, asking him what was so wrong that had him in such hysterics. He couldn't answer her, he was laughing so much. And he was fine with that. He was perfectly fine to just keep on laughing and laughing on through the night and into tomorrow.

Why not laugh? He'd never been so damned happy to simply be alive.

Vegas Moon

He sat at the bus-stop, hunched over and soul aching beneath the flickering sheen of fluorescent lights. A hint of cigarette smoke hung in the air, bringing to mind the threat of everlasting fire. He stared down at his hands. They hung there, limp between his knees. They wouldn't stop shaking.

My God, Matthew kept repeating in his head. *My God, please forgive me . . .*

They were old hands, marked by blooming liver spots and wrinkled by the years they'd held. He'd thought they had lost their strength long ago, that now they were good for little more than flipping through pages and shaking in shows of fervor. But tonight's travesty had proven otherwise. They still had might, still had grip—could still kill, given the proper, desperate circumstance. And they had. God in Heaven, help him—they had.

It'd taken him ten whole minutes to wash the blood from his fingers. They were clean now, but they weren't pure. No amount of scrubbing could make it so. He wanted to weep at the knowledge of it. Although, come to think of it, they hadn't been pure for quite some time now. He'd dealt his sins like cards and they had led him to this exact, horrible outcome: all in, and with murder upon his shoulders.

Lord, help me.

He glanced over to the teenager sitting on the opposite end of the bench. She was the only other soul in sight, waiting here for the bus that would take them out of the city. She wore a beanie, her dark and unkempt hair falling out from under it. Her rail-thin arms were covered by a long-sleeved shirt (with something called My Chemical Romance on it); it seemed an odd choice of attire, given the rather warm evening. She'd wrapped those twiggy appendages around her backpack while her shadow-streaked eyes looked longingly up into the sky. He followed their arch, looking up towards the mammoth moon that claimed the hazy Las Vegas sky. Its face was full and tinged with a peculiar orange-red, a faint ring of the off-kilter color encircling the heavenly body like a halo.

He thought he'd heard people call that a blood moon. At the recollection, he looked back down to his hands.

The young man had been waiting for him as he headed home. Matthew hadn't known him, hadn't ever seen him around before, much less knew his name; he wasn't sure if that made matters better or worse. He'd stepped out of the shadows of the street and waltzed up to Matthew, a welcoming smile on his face. Matthew had greeted him with equal cheer.

"Nice night, ain't it?" the youth had said. Matthew had agreed, and vehemently so.

"A perfect night to take a walk, just breathe in the air. See the strip and the rest of the town . . . or maybe go down to The Black Spot and place a bet. One you can't cover."

Matthew had been at a loss for words after this, his fear rising up swift and sudden as a tide.

"Mr. Ricci has given you plenty of chances to pay up all that you owe him. And, stupid you, you haven't forked up a cent. Rather than squeeze you for it, the boss sent me to make an example of you."

The young man's hand had slipped into his coat pocket, and it came back out with a glinting knife. He held it low to his waist, the wicked tip aimed towards Matthew's gut.

"Cut the old fucker open. His words, not mine."

The young man's arm shot out, and to Matthew's astonishment, his own were just as quick, rising up to grasp the man's wrist and elbow. The youth was obviously surprised by the show of defense, and more so by the strength Matthew displayed as he tried wrenching the knife from the hired killer's hand. The two slammed into each other, the younger man bearing down on Matthew and trying to throw him aside. But Matthew was resilient, and he gave the man a harsh shake, putting all of his weight into the matter. Then, in a split second of luck (or lack thereof), the young man pulled back just as Matthew gave his arm a sharp shove, and the would-be killer let out a harsh grunt. His upper half went slack over Matthew.

The blade had been buried in his stomach, up to the hilt, a dark red spilling out over the youth's shirt. He'd looked Matthew dead in the eye as he gave a floundering gasp, and then he fell, lying sideways on the darkened sidewalk, dead.

A world's worth of terror came falling down on Matthew in that moment, a hundred choices and actions rushing through his mind, tormenting him, taunting him. What was he to do?

If he reported the matter, he *might* be shown leniency by the law, maybe even be put in some sort of protection from Donald Ricci and his underlings; but his life would be ruined, all the same, and his name with it.

He couldn't just walk away and act like it'd never happened; even if he was never caught and arrested for the deed, Ricci would just send another thug after him—maybe worse.

Maybe if he ran . . . skipped town, as they said in the movies . . . maybe . . .

Though it'd felt like an eternity of internal debate, only a few moments had passed before Matthew started walking away, looking around to see if any possible witnesses were about. Satisfied enough that there weren't any, Matthew had walked the nine blocks back to his home. Within an hour, he'd packed a bag of clothes and some food, grabbing his savings from their tin can up in his bedroom closet. Then he'd walked the better part of two miles to the bus station, buying a ticket for the first bus heading out of Vegas.

A line from Proverbs had plagued him through the whole of his wait: "The wise will inherit honor, but fools display dishonor." And Matthew felt beyond foolish; but the great shame of it would not dissuade him. This was the only choice that afforded him some sense of freedom. He only hoped that, with time and prayer and good deeds, he would be freed of his guilt by God's decree.

Freeing himself from that guilt, however . . .

A forceful hissing brought Matthew out of his thoughts. A bus was sidling up to the curb, its brakes giving a squeak as it came to a harsh stop. The teenager across from Matthew stood up and slung her backpack over her shoulder as the bus' door slid open. She trudged past him, her eyes down to her shoes. She stepped up to the door, pausing as she looked up to the driver. She half-turned about; there was a worrisome look on her face. She glanced to Matthew while her fingers tapped at the strap of her backpack. Then she turned back around, trudging up the steps and taking a seat close to the front.

Matthew looked back up to that moon, wondering if God was looking down on him from somewhere far beyond it. Very far.

As he took in that strange red hue, his hand rose up to the neck of his shirt. His fingers slipped around his white clerical collar. He gave it a tug and it snapped free.

The fluorescents overhead flickered as he grabbed hold of his bag. He set the collar down on the bench and stood up. He wouldn't need it, wherever he was going.

***

Matthew was administering communion in a far grander church than his own; indeed, far grander than he'd ever laid eyes on, with a vaulted ceiling of stone and a congregation that stretched back for half a mile's worth of pews. A thousand beaming faces looked up at him in admiration. Their forms were haloed in the glimmering light of the glorious day, the glow seeping through the towering stained-glass windows overhead. Each attendant held a hand to their heart as Matthew went along a line of standing youths, bestowing the body and the blood of Christ to each.

He had let ten or so Communicants sip from the cup before he bothered to realize it was actual blood that had been meeting their lips, and how they swallowed it so very happily.

The realization did not bother him though, and he saw to his duty with the steadfastness of faith—until he came to a rather sad looking boy, swaying to and fro, as if in a daze. His eyes were sunken and his hair was tousled, and it seemed that all the fear of the world was etched upon his features. Matthew told him to have no fear, but the boy still looked forlorn as he took the cup and drank.

When Matthew tried to pull the cup away, the boy would not let it go.

From over the lip, his sad eyes began to narrow, his throat trembling as he madly slurped away. The youth gave a sharp tug and Matthew's grip failed, the blood from the cup spilling out across the boy's face and suited breast as he downed the last of it.

And then it happened.

The boy was no longer a boy. In an instant he had become the young man Matthew had murdered, skin pale, shirt soaked and sagging with red.

He stared up at Matthew with a sadist's grin, his breathing ragged and his eyes showing a sick satisfaction. No, not at Matthew—at something over his shoulder. Mathew turned, a cry of horror catching in his throat as he saw.

The dead man was looking up to the grand crucifix hanging before the proceedings. But it was not a silent and wooden Christ who'd been nailed to it, as it should have been; it was Matthew himself, alive and screaming and sleeked in sweat and the blood which trickled from his crowned brow and which poured out his side—exactly where the son of God had been pierced. Exactly where he had driven the knife into the young man.

As his suffering doppelgänger screamed on, Matthew finally let loose his own cry, though to his ears, it sounded more like the screeching of tires . . .

And it was the screeching of the bus' tires that woke him—just before a thunderous crash of metal rang out and the whole of the bus went tipping over.

Matthew's world went sideways as he was launched out of his seat. His left hip smacked sharply into the armrest, spinning him about as he tumbled down towards the seats across the aisle. His temple whacked into a headrest, the pain of it barely registering amid the chaos. His arms tried to grab hold of the seat as the side of the bus slammed into dark pavement, the windows that were now beneath him shattering and spitting out in a hail. The bus screeched and ground along as Matthew fought to catch himself, kicking his legs out at the seats ahead, trying to hoist his body across them, lest his head go smacking and tearing against the road that went grinding by in the window beneath him.

He managed to keep himself from falling until the bus came to a rest, and then the strength went out of his limbs. He tipped over, his back careening down into the sprinkles of glass that covered the side of the overturned bus.

He lay there for a minute, his body numb, but his heart tight and wild in his chest. He fought to breath. Fought to even think. His sight went dark for a minute and he let his head hit the steel underneath him.

When he came back around, the clinch in his chest had eased and he could feel his limbs again. And they ached. Groaning, his head now throbbing from its blow, he fought to get up. He grabbed hold of a seat and hauled himself up, draping his chest across it as he stood. He shook his head to clear it, little bits of glass flinging from the tufts of his graying hair.

He felt dizzy as he took in the topsy-turvy bus. The seat he'd occupied now loomed over his head. Dim moonlight snuck in from the windows, falling upon the seats above and casting long shafts of shadow through the bus' shambled guts. Looking towards the front, Matthew saw how the right corner had been nearly caved in, the metal jutting inwards like a collapsed awning and the doors hanging down by ruined hinges. The great big windshield was a web-work of smashed glass; one flick of a finger would set it to raining down. Things were eerily quiet, save for a dripping sound that came *plink-plink-plink*ing through the bus' underside and a soft groaning that hid somewhere in the shadows.

It took a moment for the significance of the groaning to hit Matthew. When it did, he moved up towards the front, using the seats for purchase, his banged-up hip screaming at him to take it slow. Through the dimness, he could see a pair of thin legs stretched out in one of the aisles ahead. A sneakered foot was twitching. When he reached the girl who'd boarded with him, he knelt down and made to help her. But his words of assurance got caught up in his mouth and stayed put.

She was trembling all over, her bloodied and beanieless head leaning against what had once been the floor. Judging by the glass-speckled cavity in her left temple, she'd fallen right into one of the windows in the midst of the crash. Strings of her sleeked hair dipped into the wound, clinging to the torn flesh. Matthew grabbed her hand; he fought to look her in the eye and not at that sickening hole in her head. She didn't return the gaze—she just stared off into space, her hand tightening around his. When she spoke, Matthew wasn't even sure she was speaking to him.

"I didn't . . . didn't wanna go . . ."

Matthew nodded, as if he understood. She was so pale and turning paler by the second. He set his other hand to her arm, trying to keep it from trembling so. The sleeve had been pulled up, a dark bruise showing beneath the crook of her elbow.

"I didn't wanna . . . leave you, Mama . . . but I . . . *told* you."

Tears welled up in her eyes and fell down her cheek, trailing along a bit of blood that'd already trickled the same path. Her voice was the whimper of a baby's.

"I . . . I *showed* you. Why wouldn't you . . . ?"

Matthew hated that look in her eyes, and his own darted down. Enough moonlight was creeping in to where he could see a tear in her shirt, just over her ribs. A yellow-green bruise stood out beneath the material. Matthew was sure that she hadn't gotten it in the crash.

"I didn't wanna . . . didn't wanna . . ."

The girl gave a pained lurch, her plea trailing into rapid huffs of breath. And though he'd never done it before, Matthew's thumb was up to her head in an instant, signing a cross, and then the words were out of his mouth, shaky but quick.

"Our Father who art in Heaven, hallowed be thy name. Thy kingdom come, thy will be done, on earth as it is in Heaven. Give us . . ."

The image of his collar, abandoned at the bus-stop, flashed into his mind.

The prayer fell short, his recitation of the last rites hindered as guilt slammed down upon him like a press. He tried to continue, but it just wouldn't come. It couldn't.

He was not a good man anymore—much less a man of God. Why would He hear him now? What right did he have to speak these words, to pray for a life when he had ended another? Was that simple hypocrisy or near-lunacy, to have those hopes upon his tongue?

As he pondered this, the girl's trembling fell away. It wasn't until her hand slipped out of his loosened grip that

Matthew realized she was gone—having faded like the sole bit of comfort he might have given her.

He looked at his hand a moment longer and then stood.

He let loose a pent-up breath and moved further to the front, craning his head to check on the driver. The man hung about in his seat like some marionette, the seat-belt pinching around his pudgy torso. His wide-eyed face was marked by lacerations; bits of glass pricked out of his pinkish face, red drops slipping and dripping off of them.

A wave of claustrophobia swelled over Matthew, the twisted metal and dark spaces closing in on him. He spun back around and made for the emergency hatch set into the transport's roof. He gave its latch a tug. Its cover fell outwards, clanging across the road. He hunched over and hauled himself out, taking a deep breath of the chilled desert air.

A shadowed vista stretched out to either side of the two-lane road, the edge of the crumbling asphalt giving way to miles and miles of red dirt and brush. Matthew could see up to a mile off under that red-orange moonlight, but anything past that was covered by indistinct shadow or lost in the lumbering darkness of mountains in the beyond. There were no other vehicles in sight—save for the other bus that had crashed into theirs—and no headlights off in the distance, nor were there any signposts or buildings or anything to indicate where they might be in the whole wide state of Nevada.

Matthew's mouth went dry as he took the night in, his tongue a lump of mulch between his teeth. He mustered up some spittle as he stepped towards the other bus—still upright, but its front end mangled, much like their own. He called out to anyone inside who might hear him. He waved his arm out at its shattered front window. No one waved back. He crept around and up to its doors, looking in at the driver lying across the steering wheel, wrinkled face knotted up in what had once been pain. He looked unharmed to Matthew's eyes, and he wondered if the man had suffered a heart-attack in light of the crash. Or maybe he'd had one beforehand; perhaps in his pain, he'd lost control of the bus and sent it crashing into theirs, leaving them all to this.

Matthew sidled along the side of the bus, trying to catch a glimpse of anyone else inside. He called out again, but still no one answered, and there was nothing but blank space beyond every window. There had been no one else on board. A small consolation, Matthew supposed, but it was something.

He turned back around, glancing to his bus and seeing the hanging driver past the cracked window. He quickly averted his eyes, turning them down to the blacktop. Then he stood there, feeling the weight of choice bearing down on him yet again, and bemoaning how terrible it was. What was he to do now? A normal person in normal circumstances would have gotten out a cell phone and called for help; that seemed the logical move. But Matthew wasn't in the midst of normal circumstances and he had no cell phone of his own. He imagined the girl in the bus might have one (what teenager these days didn't?) but the notion of searching her body or her things set Matthew's stomach to roiling beyond his liking. And—though he loathed himself to think it—what good would it do to call authorities? The dead were dead—God help them. And he was on the run—God forgive him.

Authorities would bring questions he couldn't bear to answer, and that, in turn, would bring him right back to all he had so desperately fled from. But, again, what else was he to do?

The answer, it seemed, was the same as he had already been doing: just run. Grab his bag, flee another scene, and walk the road until something presented itself. And if someone came upon him? Well, he was just a hitchhiker making his way to see family in some other state, huffing it as far and as well as he could, and would you by chance be able to give me a little lift or point me to a bus station? Or, on second thought, know of a cab service, instead? Questions would be asked and suspicions raised, no doubt, but as long as the curious party didn't have a badge on their person, Matthew could take it.

"Someone will be by soon enough," Matthew whispered. "Surely they will."

Someone who could notify whoever needed notifying of the accident, and they would see to the poor souls involved, and no one need ever be the wiser that Matthew had any involvement in the matter. No one need know how he talked to the girl, how she stared up at him, how he held her hand as she . . .

Matthew groaned, his eyes burning. But he'd already decided what to do, and now he had only to do it. *And live with it*, his conscience reminded him.

He rubbed the arm of his jacket across his eyes as he walked back over to his bus, taking steady breaths before he crept back inside. He searched for his bag, his hands darting through the darkness until they found it. Then he crept back out, averting his eyes from the girl.

He looked down the long stretch of road that lay ahead. And then he started walking.

***

It'd been over thirty years ago and nearly two thousand miles away when Matthew went to Father Walsh about his plans. He'd already considered the matter for a good while, but he wanted the Father's opinion before he decided for good.

He'd come to value the priest's opinion over any other's in those last few years. He'd become his spiritual advisor, a mentor—hell, an honest to God friend. Matthew had told him his greatest fears and confessed his every sin to the man; had told him about his dip into the drugs and his stint of running questionable packages for the Chicago Outfit in his teens. But he'd also shown him his newfound love of God and the changes it'd made ever since he chose to "get right," finding a steady job, working through college, and involving himself more and more with the church. And because of that, there was nobody who knew him better, and nobody better to give him the odds and an honest evaluation.

They'd gone out for a late lunch one breezy day, followed up by a stroll through Jackson Park. Matthew had finally worked up the nerve to bring up seminary school near the end of their meal. He'd poured out his intentions and worries, spitting up hours of internal debate and letting Walsh chew it over, along with the rest of his burger. By the time they'd left the diner and meandered to the Osaka Gardens, the priest had still yet to say anything about the matter.

Finally, Matthew couldn't take wondering anymore. "So, what do you think?" he'd asked.

Father Walsh had looked up to the sky, squinting under the sunlight, and shrugged. "I think that if the Cubs don't win the series this year, I'll be reconsidering atheism."

Matthew couldn't help but grin. "That's not exactly what I'm getting at."

"No," the priest said, stepping up to a fancy bridge with an oriental flare. He leaned over the railing and looked down to the trickling stream below. "I'm just a sucker for a long shot."

Matthew had sidled up alongside him, grasping at the hint. He hadn't been sure if he cared for it. "And you think I'm a long shot, too. That I'm wasting my time even considering seminary."

Walsh had shaken his head after a bit of consideration.

"A long shot, maybe. A waste of time? Absolutely not. You want to serve something bigger than yourself, to devote yourself to a cause, and I don't think that's ever a waste. And you did well in college, you've shown an aptitude and interest in the church—that's all in your favor, in the eyes of any seminary. But if you're wanting to know whether or not I think you'd make a good priest . . ."

He'd shaken his head again and flicked a stray breadcrumb off the rail, down into the green waters below.

"I don't know. I just don't. I've known priests that could talk the Pope under the table about all things theology, but when a member of their church came to them for advice, they completely froze. On the other hand, I've met priests who hardly knew their Luke from their John, but who could—and did—reshape whole lives with a few loving words. Some really can't do either, but still live their whole lives with the collar around their necks. Then, there are those who give it a try, and it doesn't suit them and they leave the church after a year or so, what have you. The thing is, outside looking in, you can never really tell which one a man will become. Which is why I can't give you the answer I think you want."

Matthew had taken this all in silently and gravely, as a pupil before the headmaster. So gravely, perhaps, that Father Walsh had seen the worry on his face; the old man had clapped a hand on his shoulder as though to ease him.

"You're asking me which road you'll end up taking when you're the one behind the wheel. It's up to you. Your determination—your faith, however great it is—will ultimately decide. But, I have to say . . ." And he'd smiled at Matthew when it came to this: "I imagine you have a fine road ahead of you."

***

In his years since being ordained, Matthew had often thought back to Father Walsh's words on that long-off day. And now, wandering through the Nevada desert with the moon to his back, he couldn't help but think on them again, try as he might not to.

A fine road. Matthew could almost laugh at that, given his current circumstances. But he didn't. He just kept walking, feeling as lost as ever and in every sense of the word.

He'd left the bus behind—thirty, maybe forty minutes ago? Maybe even less than that. It was impossible to tell for sure out here, without a watch. However long, it'd already felt interminable. And he'd yet to see a car or trucker pass by in either direction, and there still hadn't been any signs or exits giving him a clue of where he was. It was just him out here, his steps echoing out into the vast nothing, not even a dessert critter scurrying just off the roadside, coming out to feed or stare at the lone man with the hunched shoulders and downcast face.

Matthew kicked a stray chunk of asphalt off the road, still stewing in his thoughts of the past.

For a long shot, he'd thought he'd actually hit the mark. He managed to get into Mundelein and excelled in his studies. It was a grueling process, but he'd adapted and rose to the task. Four years later he'd graduated and brought his diploma to Father Walsh, who'd gone into the hospital by then with severe pneumonia. The poor man had looked like hell in that bed, skinny and trembling, half-alive and half-awake, but he'd brandished a big smile when he saw Matthew.

"Still waiting on the Cubs," he'd whispered.

He passed two weeks later, just before Matthew decided for good to head out west. In fact, it was his mentor's passing that cinched it; there was little else holding him to Chicago.

He'd figured he'd set his old life right and it was time to start a new one, and in a new place, away from the memories and alleys of his old stomping ground. The archdiocese had allowed for his reassignment and he'd lit out for Vegas soon after, figuring there'd be plenty calling for his new role. Not the best of places for him to go, especially in recent retrospect, but at the time he'd felt like a veritable warrior of God, ready to lead wayward souls and sink his teeth into the city's sin and give it a shake. And for a good while, he felt he was doing just that with his parish, spreading the Word and bringing community with it. Fool that he was, he hadn't realized how wayward *he* still was, or how his own sins would leave behind the needles for a phone in their stead, making calls to bookies.

Thanks to his youth, he knew how the shadier elements moved and where to seek them out, and he'd eventually found the right people to go to when a big game, match, or race was coming. That's how he found Donald Ricci and The Black Spot, both of which had reputations he'd heard plenty about since coming to town. They weren't any Chicago Outfit, though, and he believed he knew how to handle their ilk.

At first, he thought it'd all been well enough; a little bet here for a little bit extra in the church's funds. And he'd had a streak of perfect picks that spurred him on further. He'd quickly justified it, the dumb bastard—far too quickly. And when he started losing and wouldn't take the hint, he ignored the walls of the hole he'd dug up and jumped into, thinking God would see him through. He'd been doing it for Him, after all. Or so he'd told himself—so he'd justified.

So, had it been God who'd forsaken him to this road, or had he just done it to himself? Either way, he had to walk it now, and . . .

As Matthew looked up into the distance, something caught his eye. Perhaps his mind was playing tricks on him, but it looked like there was a faint glow rising up through the dim haze of the horizon. He blinked and narrowed his eyes, and yes, there was some light up ahead, maybe a mile or so away. Maybe a car heading his way, maybe not, but it was the first sign of life he'd had, and Matthew quickened his pace a bit in hope.

He ignored the burn setting in through his calves and the dull throbbing of his feet, trying to solidify his story, should he have someone to tell it to. Should it be a cousin in Utah he was on his way to see, or a brother in Oregon? He supposed it didn't matter, so long as he could sell it.

After a few more minutes of walking, the lights grew stronger and more definite, and Matthew realized it wasn't a car coming, but a little gas station. The light was coming from the awning over the pumps and from within the storefront; a towering sign for the place stood out by the road, unlit but coming into clarity. He couldn't see any cars in the little lot, but if the lights were on they must have been opened; all-hours stations made sense out here, since populated stops were still few and far between in the great nowhere.

Matthew licked at his dried lips, feeling quite parched by now. He glanced up to the sign as he stepped over a curb and onto the pavement of the lot. The Pit Stop. Matthew figured if you took out the "Stop," the name would still fit; the place sure wouldn't pop up in any Nevada brochures, if its appearance was any indicator. It was a mom-and-pop kind of station; maybe erected in the seventies or thereabouts. "Rustic" if being polite and a "dump" if being straight-forward. It bore the marks of age and the elements, the pumps looking a little rusted and busted and the teal walls of the building faded and sandblasted. Matthew really didn't care, as long as a friendly face and a helpful hand waited inside.

A bulky ice machine hummed just outside the front doors, giving a few whines in the time it took Matthew to reach it, as though it were close to breaking down. The poor thing was probably as old as he was.

When he opened the door and stepped into the store, a little bell jingled overhead, cutting into the verse of a Tammy Wynette song. It was playing on a beat-up radio sitting on the counter to his left. No one was at the register, some worker's Big-Gulp left to sweat beside it.

"Hello there?" Matthew called out. There was no answer, save for a lamenting chorus from Miss Wynette.

He paced about a bit, glancing down the few aisles to his right, their shelves bearing chips and beer cases and other amenities for the road. There were no customers in sight, or an attendant. The last aisle had a flank of fridges and freezers set into the wall, the faces of sports drinks and sodas smiling out at Matthew, each looking awfully tempting.

"Hello?" he said again, trying for a measure of cheer he didn't feel. "You've, uh . . . got a thirsty fellow who hit the road—and the road's hit back."

He gave a forced laugh as he stepped up to a freezer and plucked out a bottle of water. He snapped the cap and chugged a good bit of it, relishing the coolness.

At the end of the aisle he saw a short hall, leading to the back of the station and its loading area. Probably to a restroom, as well.

"Well, uh, I was wondering if you had a phone I could use, or knew of a cab ser—"

The fluorescent lights overhead gave a flicker, cutting him off as he glanced up to the stained ceiling. The ice machine outside gave a sharp rattle, its side banging into the station's wall, and then it let loose a pop and a groan. At the same time, the lights went out.

Ms. Wynette's song ended and the ice machine drew out a hiss until it eased, leaving the whole place in darkness and silence.

Matthew put the cap back on his water and gave a bitter laugh. Would this night ever end?

"You seem to be having some electrical troubles!"

He inched down the aisle, closer to that off-shoot hall which was now bathed in shadow, save for a shaft of moonlight coming from a window across the way. The linoleum cracked and creaked under his feet, the only noise in the still-dark, until something else reached his ear. It was a soft thumping, repeating about every two or three seconds—and from somewhere down the hall.

"You okay back there?" Matthew called. He figured maybe the attendant was bumbling around in the restroom, trying to find his or her way out in the dark, smacking into stuff. But why hadn't they answered him yet?

He stepped down the aisle and reached the hall. The thumping was growing a tad louder. It was coming from his right, beyond a doorway with a sign nailed to it; in the dim moonlight, it looked like it read "Ye Olde Throne." Matthew knocked on the door.

"Anyone in there?"

He didn't get an answer. The thumping continued.

Bracing himself for an embarrassing intrusion, Matthew pushed the door open and peeked inside. A grimy window across the room let in just enough light to see by, revealing a plain but relatively tidy restroom. The walls were covered in splashes of cracked white and beige, and the floor was only a little bit sticky. There was a sink and a mirror in the immediate left corner. A urinal hung on the adjoining wall, and to its right, nestled in the far corner, was a stall. Its door was cracked open, swung in a couple inches, and the thumping was coming from within its walls.

Matthew stepped up to the stall, clearing his throat out of nervousness—and as a warning to anyone inside. When no one hollered at him to get the hell out, he pushed the door open and cautiously looked inside.

A young woman sat on the toilet, dressed in a short skirt and a tight top, her face hidden under scraggily black hair as she banged her forehead against the wall—the source of the thumping. She was whispering words that Matthew couldn't quite make out, the hiss of some frantic recitation. Not quite a prayer, but just as desperate. Even in the darkness, her pale skin looked odd, like it was covered in a fine dusting of dirt and smudge.

She cradled a trembling hand in her lap; a marker of some sort was dancing in her twitching fingers.

The walls around her were nearly covered in black, and it wasn't from the shadows. It was ink. She had drawn across the brick walls and the aluminum of the stall, covering nearly every possible inch and leaving her as the center of some stormy scene of chaos. There were words here and there, just barely discernible amid the random swoops and scratches of angry lines. Matthew could make out a few choice scrawls ("HE IS GONE" and "GIVE ME BACK TO ME" stood out in big bold letters), but most of it was lost to him.

The woman's whispers steadily trailed off. She began to cry, her nose sniffling and her lips sucking in harsh snags of air. She finally rested her head against the wall and shook with her sorrow.

"Ma'am, are you—?"

Her head shot up and she focused a cutting glare at him. Her eyes seemed to glow amid her mask of unwashed filth. She turned her lip up at him, sneering.

"I told you to leave me alone!" she said through bared teeth. "Stay *away* from me! I don't want any more of that *shit*!"

She brandished her marker like it was a knife, jabbing it out at him while leaning back against the toilet, trying to back up to the wall. Spittle flew from her mouth as she heaved her breaths.

She screamed. "*Never. Ever. Again!*"

Matthew stepped back quickly, hands raised to show that he meant no harm. He nearly fell down when he backed into something that shouldn't have been there.

He wheeled around and came face to face with a man that was a full head taller than him, broad-shouldered, and reeking of something that Matthew couldn't place. How the man had snuck into the room without his noticing—by the size or the smell of him—was beyond Matthew.

The man wore a stained work-shirt with the name of "Randy" on its breast-tag. His bearded mug opened wide in a smile that was missing a few teeth, and the ones that were there had rotted and yellowed. He gave a goofy chuckle as Matthew turned away from him and away from the still-yelling woman, backing up to the door that led back into the station.

The lummox—Randy—turned his head down all of a sudden, like some irate bull. His smile switched into a look of menacing severity. He looked back to the stall, his huge chest rising and falling in excitement as he looked to the woman.

When he charged at her, and as she screamed again, Matthew turned, flinging the door open and barreling out into the hall.

Fear compelled his legs as he stumbled through the dark, crashing into a stand of sunglasses before zipping down the aisle and then back out into the night.

He ran back out to the road and then kept on running, not daring to look back.

***

Matthew had no clue just how far he'd gone before he finally had to slow, but when he forced himself to glance back, the gas station was nowhere in sight. Still, he kept on, wanting to put as much distance between himself and the Pit Stop as he could, no matter how his legs and chest burned from exertion.

He kept going a little ways longer, perhaps another quarter mile, before the hitch in his step got to be too much—and until something of note came into sight just up ahead.

It was a lone, rusted stop sign. It leaned in the dirt, at the corner of what had once been a four-way stop, another stretch of road cutting its way through the dark landscape. Matthew peered to either horizon, looking for headlights, but still there were none.

He tossed his backpack onto the edge of the road and set himself down in the dirt, leaning his back against the sign's pole, desperately needing a rest. It would've done him well to get a snack of something from his provisions, but he didn't feel up to eating. Not after what had just happened—whatever the hell it had even been.

Matthew struggled to understand what the girl had been on about and how "Randy" had just shown up like he did, but it was all too wild for him to put right. And his own actions, just running like he had—that should have born some serious consideration. But he would not allow it. He could not. He forced that nagging bit of conscience aside and focused on the dirt before him, making himself think on what was to come next instead of what had already passed.

Would he continue on down the road he'd been on? Or should he take one of the crossroads? There were still no other signs to tell if any populations were in reach, nor glows in either distance to indicate nearby cities. Truthfully, there was nothing at all to distinguish one way from another. Each looked to be a paltry choice; Matthew ground his teeth, realizing just how well that applied to all his crossroads this night.

He eventually put his head in his hands and just sat there, shutting his eyes and trying his best to think nothing at all. It worked, for a time. But then a something came intruding upon the nothing; the sound of scratchy footsteps along asphalt came to his ears, and though he doubted the truth of the noise, at first, it was steadily growing louder. Closer.

Matthew glanced to his left. The rosy light of the moon revealed the surprising sight of an elderly man walking his way. He was shuffling along down the middle of the road, his feet hardly rising before lunging forward, step after labored step. He was quietly moaning and groaning what might have been words, although Matthew couldn't make them out. But the look on his weathered face was unmistakable; it was anguish.

Matthew watched as the man went right on by him; he had never even seemed to notice him sitting there. But as the man reached the center of the crossroads, he gave a stumble forward, and Matthew was spurred into action, fearing that the traveler was on the verge of falling face-first into the asphalt.

"Wait," Matthew called to the man. He'd righted himself and kept on going, but he was still unsteady. "Please, wait up!"

Matthew forced his way ahead of the man and set his hands to his bony shoulders, forcing him to halt. The stranger still tried to go along, as though Matthew was hardly there, but he turned his eyes up to look him in the eye. His beard and denim clothes were covered in a fine dusting of dirt, the wrinkles of his face looking like cracks along a desert floor. He might have been in his seventies, and by the reek of him, one would think he hadn't bathed in the last ten of those years. Matthew pulled back a bit, wincing against the smell, but he kept his grip strong.

"Sir, are you okay?" It seemed a stupid question, but Matthew had to wonder if the man was even present enough to communicate.

The older man just blinked up at him for a moment, his eyes growing misty. When he spoke, it was an aged garble, made all the more tremulous by his haggard state.

"After all I did for him. Raising him, feeding him . . ."

The man shook his head, his mouth pulling back and past his teeth in an ugly look of sorrow. His breaths started to hitch.

"Then he was gone. Just . . . left! But I . . . I found him. And I huffed all the way to Utah! Just to see him! To say I loved him. Even if he didn't love me no more!"

The man looked down to the road, tears plopping onto the tops of his worn boots.

"He . . . wouldn't even let me in . . . w-wouldn't even *listen* . . ."

The man pulled away from Matthew, shaking off his grasp with the strength of his emotions.

"*I'm his father, damn it*!" he shouted out to the dark. "I gave him life . . . I loved him . . . And he wouldn't let me in."

He started to stumble away, heading on down the road, leaving Matthew to stand there, arms out to his sides and hands opened in an uncertainty of what to do.

Matthew was so focused on the sad stranger, it took him a moment to recognize the sound of a rumbling engine coming along, and to realize there were headlights drawing near them, down the road to his right.

A bit of hope sparked to life inside Matthew.

"Hold up, sir!" He turned around and darted back to the stop sign and his backpack. "Let's see if we can get a ride from this person and then get you some help . . ."

The man's shuffling steps kept up as the car's lights fell along the road. "I still don't even know why he left . . ."

Matthew bent over and grabbed his things as the sound of brakes squeaked over his shoulder.

"Thank you!" he shouted out, overjoyed that someone had come along, hoping the driver could hear him and that they could get him far away from here. "Thank you so much for stopping! It means a great deal to—"

He heard one of the car doors opening, and then another. Then there was laughter—from a few different people, and it somehow sounded . . . wrong. Someone spat onto the road, and then there was a metallic *clink* against the asphalt.

"Lookee what we got here," a youthful voice said. "One of them double-down deals!"

Matthew straightened and turned back around, the light of his hope already flickering.

A beat-up '64 Impala sat on the side of the road a few yards away, its engine grumbling like a sleeping giant. Its paint job betrayed its years, the old cherry hue nearly sun-bleached to pink, wherever it wasn't rusted or scratched up. Its two doors were opened; a young man had slipped out on the right side, fingers tapping along the roof while another sat in the backseat, staring out with a look of pure glee on his pimpled mug. The driver and the passenger—two other young men—were standing in front of the car. All four were dressed in white t-shirts and blue jeans, their hair sleeked up with grease. The passenger boy had a leather jacket on for variety—and he was leaning on the aluminum baseball bat in his grip. The grinning driver had one of his own, cradled up and over his shoulder.

"It looks like we got ourselves two innings, Petey," the passenger said. He kicked his bat, swinging it up and grasping it in both hands.

"So it does, Hank," the driver agreed; it'd been he who spoke up the moment before. His voice still had a sick mirth to it. "Don't you just love game night?"

"Primo, old buddy. Primo."

They advanced on the old man, who kept walking up to them, mumbling his sad words.

"Spitowski's up at bat first!" the passenger shouted into the night, using a brazen announcer's voice. The other two boys started cheering and whooping behind him as he raised his bat, readying a swing.

A plea blared in Matthew's mind, but his lips went slack.

"There's the pitch! The swing! And . . ."

Matthew went cold as the boy swung the bat right into the old man's chest, the aluminum connecting with a harsh *thwack*. The man hollered in pain and stumbled backwards, arms hugging his chest.

"A straight pop up center-field!"

The four boys chuckled as the old man turned away from them, crumpling into himself as new tears fell from his eyes. The driver hesitated for just a moment, and then he readied his own bat, sneaking slowly up to the old man.

"Mathers is up next!" he called. "Can he live up to last season?"

He swung with all his might. The bat's tip went cracking into the back of the old man's head. A spurt of red shot up from his skull and he fell straight down into a still pile.

"Ooh, a ground ball!" the driver-boy moaned in mock dismay.

He and his friend stepped over to either side of the man and raised their bats. They brought them down in a mad flurry, their friends cheering louder, while Matthew was still riveted in place with terror.

"The Carson City Crushers are on fire tonight, folks!"

The boys pummeled the old man, hitting every square inch of his body over and over, the sounds of bones breaking striking up, along with the hits from the bats. Matthew lost count of how many times they struck; the whole awful matter seemed to just go on and on.

"That was one hell of an inning, friends!" the passenger said as they finally started to slow, catching their breath.

The driver beamed and wiped a forearm over his face. "Schenkel couldn't put it any better, Hank-o."

They took a few steps back, taking in their handiwork. The man didn't move or whimper in the least. He just laid there, his body twisted up and broken.

"Second inning!" the pimply boy in the car hooted. "Keep it going!"

The driver and the passenger looked over to Matthew. They smiled at him.

Matthew finally turned and ran, fleeing out into the dust of the desert. His backpack slipped from his fingers, but it was no matter to him. He just yelled and sped up.

"Round up time!" one of the boys hollered. "*Sooee!*"

"Pin the Pig, boys! Pin the Pig!"

The others took up the cry; a moment later, Matthew heard the Impala's doors slam shut and its engine revving. The squeal of tires rose up like a siren's cry and the shine of the headlights turned upon Matthew's back, his flailing shadow running along ahead of him. There was a wrenching sound as the car's nose smashed into the stop sign, running it over as the tires launched into the dirt. And the chase was on.

Matthew darted around cacti and vaulted over bushes. The *vroom* of the old car was a lion's hungry rumble that filled his ears. He could hear the vehicle swerving about, the driver trying to avoid the jutting rocks sprinkled along the landscape. Matthew glanced back now and again, when it seemed the car's nose was closest to his heels, only to face forward once more, desperately seeking somewhere and some way to escape his pursuers.

The car would lurch up towards him only to fall back, playing with him. The boys kept up their jeers and the swine calls; their racket only ever quieted when another good push on the gas rose up and over their voices.

Time and distance became moot for Matthew; he might have only ran for a minute—maybe even five, for all he knew—and no matter how far he managed to pull ahead of the car, it wasn't enough. There was nowhere for him to go out here.

He wailed when he tripped over his feet, falling right down into the dirt.

The car bore down on him as the tears came. And then—

Matthew hugged the dirt as the underside of the car went zooming by overhead. He had fallen into a ditch that was just long and wide enough to shelter him, but not by much; he could feel the heat of the engine upon his neck and smell the car's oily innards. It gave a hard jostle as the tires spun over the curved lip of the ditch; the boys gave an instant round of cheers overhead.

"You squashed that cat, Petey!"

The Impala's bumper cut the air over Matthew's ear, the back tires spitting dirt over him, and it went on going. Matthew kept cradling his head as the car sped off, the boys' cursing and congratulations to each other quickly turning to whispers in the night.

After checking to see that his limbs were all still there, Matthew got onto all fours, taking shallow breaths as he peered across the desert.

The Impala was already several dozen yards off. The tail-lights sparked red as the driver braked and turned the wheel, the car cutting off and heading to the right, back towards the roads. In a matter of seconds, it was out of sight, only a haze of dust left in its wake.

Matthew tried to stand, but his legs gave. He fell back onto his bottom at the edge of the ditch. He didn't try to get back up.

He sat there, shaking, hands clenching around the knees of his pants, heart still thumping and his head filled with a static mess. He swallowed down his fears, letting them settle and digest in his gut.

After a while, he hauled himself back up, and he stayed up. He stumbled out of the ditch and stood there, looking all about but barely registering the scenery.

When he moved along, he did so slowly, and in the direction that the car had gone, off to find the other road. The image of the beaten old man lying on the asphalt a ways back hung in his mind's eye like a horrid snapshot, but Matthew couldn't muster a thought as to whether or not he could help him, or whether he was still alive or not. And

Matthew's abandoned backpack would remain as such, all his remaining possessions and petty cash utterly forgotten amidst the evening's chaos.

He wouldn't go back. He'd keep on. Get back to the road and out of this damned desert. Find people. Normal people; good people. Someone that would help.

People that aren't like me, a voice bemoaned in the back of his mind. But he ignored its sorrow, trudging on through the dirt while that still-red moon lit his way.

***

Matthew kept his eyes to the sky as he walked along the roadside. It seemed that no matter how far or how long he trekked, the moon stayed in the same spot up in those dark heavens.

It had yet to descend in the least, by his gauging. He looked up to it with a longing stare, as though his meager will could force it to fall away and bring the morning, to end a night that seemed so terribly endless. He remembered wondering if God was looking on him from beyond that moon, back at the bus-stop. Now—out here, where all was empty save for pain and dust—he felt he had his answer.

Yes, God was watching; and His eyes yearned for a far better sight than Matthew.

The miles continued to be secretive ones; there had been no other roads or paths that branched off of this one, no signs to guide the traveling, and no gas stations or stop-offs to have a rest or seek out aid. If it continued that way, Matthew was sure he'd go mad. Or perhaps he already had and hadn't bothered to realize it. Maybe that was the hollowing sensation that'd been going on inside his head. Perhaps madness wasn't a chaotic frenzy in one's mind, as one might expect—some cacophonous crash of emotion and tortured thought. Maybe it was the leaving of that all, instead; a gradual fade of the ability to think or care at all, of what one knew as their essential self. An emptiness. Like this desert.

Even Shakespeare had written that "Hell is empty." Matthew couldn't help but wonder if the bard was on to something there; and if Matthew could take it a half-step forward, he'd say that Hell—at least the metaphorical kind, if nothing else—was just plain emptiness.

So—

A soft wind stirred, blowing into Matthew's face. It brought the punch of a rotten smell with it.

It was enough to cut into his mind and force him to slow, making him hold his arm up to his nose. He started hacking, folding forward for a moment as he calmed.

When he righted himself, he looked to the edge of the road, expecting a fair bit of roadkill to be lying somewhere nearby. He saw nothing of the sort, though—just more crumbling asphalt and brush. But then another breeze brought the smell back to him, and he saw a dark something fluttering beside some bushes a few feet away.

Matthew's curiosity got the better of him, and he crept ahead a bit, hand over his face. He peered around a rock and down at what looked to be a black pile of cloth, a wad just about the size of a football. He advanced a little further and the reek grew a bit stronger. When he was within reaching distance of the cloth, a swifter gust sprung up, and the flapping edge of the cloth pulled away.

The blood-crusted face of a baby lay underneath, a tiny and twisted hand curled up across its bare chest.

"*God . . . !*"

Matthew scooted back, a great big hole opening up within his chest that could only be despair. His eyes turned wet—from both the smell and the sight. He tried to look away, but no matter where his eyes turned, they kept returning to the child.

It couldn't have been more than a year old. Someone had swaddled it up only to leave it for dead. Judging by the cavity in its small skull and the dried red around it, the poor soul hadn't just been set there, either; it had been thrown, and out of a speeding car, no doubt. What monster could have . . . ?

Matthew shut his eyes tight and turned about, the question sparking another, more painful one. What monster could have done this? He had no answer for that. But what monster could just leave it like this, after the fact, allowing it to decay in the forsaken elements? That was a quandary he would now be forced to answer.

Did he see to the child, bury it as best as he could—or keep on running and call it freedom? Heaven help him, but it was a harder choice than it should have been.

After a moment of debate, he knew what he had to do. He could not turn away. Not this time. If he was to do nothing else right this night, he could—should—at least do this. He would find a place to lay the child to rest and hope that it might find some peace.

He stepped forward again, hesitantly though, keeping a hand over his mouth and nose. Then he leaned down and reached for the cloth.

A harsh snarl and the sudden rustling of brush around the baby sent Matthew darting back, his heart leaping in surprise. As soon as he recoiled, a beastly head of fur and fang came shooting out from the shadows and the bushes. Canine jaws clamped down on the baby's shoulder and pulled the limp bundle up with a shake. And then the animal was off, the child still in its mouth; Matthew caught a glimpse of a large furry rump (one that seemed much bigger than a coyote's) dashing off a yard or so ahead, and then it was gone, off to have its quick catch in solitude.

"*God damn it*!"

Matthew turned away, pacing about and heaving breaths as his legs sent him into circles and erratic stumbling.

"God . . . *God damn it all!*"

He pitched forward, falling to one knee. Moans worked their way out of his throat as he bared his teeth and stared up to the moon. His shouting eventually turned to garbled sobs.

*"*Damn it . . . damn it all!*"*

He got back up, ignoring the jolt in his scraped knee, and he started jogging away, his tears and feet falling as one along the road.

"Damn it *all* . . ."

And so he ran, and he wept, until all of his salty sorrows ran dry and his legs started to go numb from strain, and that great and terrible emptiness came back into his spirit.

The miles passed, the night remained, and the moon kept mocking him.

In his state, he hardly noticed how the breadth of the road began to narrow, closing in from either side while the blacktop became more and more cracked and degraded. It went from two lanes to one, the white lines fading away, until there was only enough room for Matthew to tread its meager path. And still he ran, and ran—until it appeared.

He finally slowed, his tears now dried and his heart light with lifelessness.

And he supposed that made sense, now that he'd finally emptied himself, allowing the truth of the night to slowly sink into his understanding.

He ambled the rest of the way, what little remained of it, for the road ended just ahead, giving way to a wide-open vista of dirt and black.

And sitting there, at the edge of the asphalt and the beyond, was a record player sitting atop a white pedestal. A vinyl record sat spinning over it, its revolutions a soft scratch against the silence of the night. It was prepped and ready, just waiting for its needle to be applied and its message heard.

Matthew stepped up to it and stopped. He stared out to the desert for a forlorn moment before looking back at the record player. With a shaky hand, he reached for the player's arm, lifting it and settling in the groove of the record. A hiss struck up from the device's speakers, and then a voice started speaking, detached and robotic, cold and uncaring. A voice of a horrible truth.

"Wash, rinse, repeat; Hell is hard on the feet. Wash, rinse, repeat; Hell is hard on the feet. Wash, rinse, repeat . . ."

Matthew hung his head and looked to his hands. They were shaking. And though they looked to be empty, they held his regret, and what a weight that was to hold onto.

What was worse, he knew that he'd be carrying it for the rest of eternity.

" . . . Hell is hard on the feet."

And then—

He sat at the bus-stop, hunched over and soul aching beneath the flickering sheen of fluorescent lights. A hint of cigarette smoke hung in the air, bringing to mind the threat of everlasting fire. He stared down at his hands. They hung there, limp between his knees. They wouldn't stop shaking.

My God, Matthew kept repeating in his head. *My God, please forgive me . . .*

The Time I Done Pranked Some Spacemen

My name's Eddie Guthrie.

I'm just a simple backwoods boy that enjoys the simple things in life—prankin' bein' chief among them. Nothing'll get me belly-laughin' quite like a good, low-down trick on someone. I've always had a knack for it, and it wasn't long until I got renowned for my larks hereabouts. Ask anyone in Bailey's Bend about me, and they'll tell you: "That Eddie Guthrie is good at only two things: taxidermy and prankin'." And boy, have I done some doozies:

I glued Blubber Davidson's butt to the seat of his '72 Explorer last summer.

I once dressed up as a zombie and stood moaning in old man Jenkins' yard; shoulda seen that doomsday prepper scootin' off to his little bunker once I started hollerin' out "Brains!"

And I was the one who put Tobasco sauce in all of the pies of the Hoyt County Fair Pie Eating Contest back in '04; even made it into the newspaper with that one.

But, by and large, the greatest darned prank I ever pulled might've just saved the world.

It sounds pretty unbelievable, I know, but here's how it all went down:

I'd just left my grandmammy's house one humid July evenin', and I was headin' on out into the swamps. I'd set up all sortsa traps out there to nab some squirrels, rabbits, whatever I could get, and it was about time I checked 'em; if I coulda caught somethin', we woulda had the meat for stew and I coulda stuffed and sold the critters. But I must have been out there for an hour, lookin' 'em over and turnin' up squat.

I was just givin' it up and headin' back home when I heard a rustlin' from the bushes around me. Sounded big enough to be a deer, but what popped out sure as hell wasn't any buck or doe.

From out of the darkness came these two gray, butt ugly aliens! Just like somethin' outta the X-Files!

Nearly made me drop a load in my shorts and jump outta my boots at the same time! Their heads were huge, like sacks of potatoes, and their eyes looked like a fly's. Their arms were these long tentacles that wiggled around like worms, their two-toed feet were bare, and they wore slicker-than-shit space suits that kinda sparkled. And they were lookin' right at me!

I was workin' up the gumption to turn tail and run when all of a sudden, they *spoke* to me—and in American!

One of 'em waved its tentacles at me and said: "Greetings, human! Be not afraid! We come bearing good tidings!"

Well, I just couldn't believe what I was seein' and hearin' yet, so I just stayed quiet.

"I am Gloth-Nar," the first spaceman said.

"And I am Zoth-Tar," the other put in.

"On behalf of our people, we wish to share our extreme pleasure in meeting you," Gloth-Nar went on. "You are the first of your species that we have encountered in our expedition of your planet. This is a momentous occasion for us, and it is no doubt surprising to you."

I still couldn't muster up a word, so I just nodded and went: "Uh-huh . . ."

Then Gloth-Nar went into a big ol' speech, tellin' me all sorts of stuff—but I only got about every other word.

"Then I shall directly detail the reasoning for our traveling to your planet and alleviate your perplexity and anxiety to the best of our capability. My comrade and I are Holoneans, from the distant planet of Holonea, and we have been sent on behalf of our people's ever expanding desire for scientific study. Ours is a culture that thrives on experimentation in all of its natures and wide possibilities, and as scientists, our particular field of interest lies in the biological process of reproduction and studies in mating."

I finally found my voice at that point, interruptin' that highfalutin spaceman.

"You mean . . . fuckin'?"

The aliens had looked at each other, thinking it over, and then Gloth-Nar nodded.

"We recognize this as one of your species' terms for the sexual act, so, in a word, yes—ours is the study of "fuuking." Specifically, we are concerned with the proposed ability and potential resulting offspring of inter-species mixing. My comrade and I have been observing your world and its multitude of organisms for a short while now, and in that time, became assured that this planet would be a suitable environment to visit and conduct our testing. We ascertained that the various life forms of this planet were profoundly promiscuous, and as such, would be likely to engage in our proposed mixings. We came to this conclusion after intercepting broadcasts of scientific studies and observations made by one of your Earth scientists, regarding your particular species' varied mating patterns."

"One Jerry Springer," Zoth-Tar added. "We found his science to be fascinating."

"As we are of the male persuasion, we are seeking out female organisms to conduct our experimental mating with. As you are a male mammal, you will clearly not suffice; however, if you could direct us towards female creatures which would be willing participants, your aid would be graciously rewarded."

"We would prefer female mammals, if you know of any," Zoth-Tar cut in again. "We find their milk-sacks to be . . . strangely alluring. However, we would settle for other female organisms, for the time being."

Gloth-Nar looked like he was noddin' at this, and he spoke up again. "And we must make you aware: if willing participants should not be found in our expedition, my comrade and I shall be forced to contact our accompanying war fleet in space; our people shall intern the Earth and *take* the subjects that are desired for copulation. Your aid can prevent this outcome."

Now, I couldn't rightly think of a single woman who'd want to accommodate these pug-ugly spacemen; not even that mattress-back Geraldine Devereux would touch 'em, and she'd damn-near touched all the fellas in town that she could. And I sure as hell couldn't abide them "interning" the world. Sounded like invasion to me, and I didn't take too kindly to that. But they had their space-hearts set on getting some human girls, and what was I to do about that?

That's when I got a devilish idea, thinkin' 'bout what we Bailey's Benders call "Chomper Central." I just hoped the aliens would be dumb enough to fall for what was startin' to brew in my head.

I said to them: "Well, I don't know of any human girls, off the top of my head. Ain't too many around in these parts. Besides . . . if you're lookin' to have some *real* fun with your experiments, it's gators that you want! You, uh . . . wouldn't happen to know nothin' about gators now, would ya?"

They looked at each other and shook their heads at me.

"Our knowledge of your world's various species *is* somewhat limited. The broadcasts we were intercepting and utilizing for research of your world were no longer attainable following a solar flare which disrupted our technology."

That got me beaming brighter than a hunter's spotlight. I said to them: "Well, gators are the horniest creatures we got on this world! They're four-legged, hang low to the ground, and like to swim. And when they ain't swimmin', they're fuckin' up a storm with one another! They've got scaly bodies and long tails and noses. Awful nice to touch! They'd be more than willin' to, uh . . . cop-u-late with ya!"

"These gators sound promising," Gloth-Nar had said. "Are there any nearby?"

"Oh, sure!" I'd smiled. "There's a whole bunch just about half a mile south of here. They just live in the woods, fuckin' all the time. They'd love to have ya!"

The aliens looked to each other again and spoke in some language I couldn't make out. After a minute of discussin' it, they spoke to me again.

"We will go to mingle with these gators and begin our experimentation. Should your suggestion prove to be worthwhile, we shall seek you out again for further recommendations. Where can we find you?"

I thought quickly and said: "Oh, you can find me right around here. I'll be waiting for ya! And just so ya know, those gators? They like to "play hard to get," as we humans say. They might not seem interested in ya, but boy, are they ever! If they hiss and bite at ya', that's their way of saying they're interested. Just go on up to 'em and woo 'em, and they'll be all over ya!"

After that, the aliens went off where I'd pointed to go, and I skedaddled on back to grandmammy's.

I stayed awake all night long, nervous and hopin' that my trick had worked—and boy, did it ever.

The next day, I went back out to the woods, right to where I'd run into those spacemen. I waited hours for them to show up like they said they would, hopin' that they wouldn't. And when they didn't, I risked goin' up to Chomper Central, where the biggest, orneriest bunch of gators these swamps have ever seen were known to hang about.

When I got there, I found quite the sight. Those two alien boys were scattered all over the edge of a marsh, their heads and arms and legs and everythin' just lyin' about, bright green blood drippin' off of everythin', torn up and half eaten. Those gators had gone and chewed 'em up!

I went back home feelin' like a hero (and carryin' some souvenirs), laughin' at the thought of those aliens tryin' to hump away at those ugly reptiles. Talk about gettin' ya some tail! And so much for "no teeth!"

I ain't seen nor heard of those aliens since that night, and our world hasn't been overrun by any UFOs lately, so I'd like to think that my trickin' those spacemen and gettin' 'em eaten up stopped their experiments and stopped their people from comin' to our planet.

Eddie Guthrie—"Prankin' Hero." I like the sound of that.

Don't believe me? Come on over to my grandmammy's house sometime! I got those aliens' heads hangin' on her basement wall!

I stuffed 'em myself.

Just Another Monday

"Well, doodie," Paul Larsen swore under his breath, hoping no one else heard the obscenity. "I'm just not sure about this."

He stared at the beneficiary change form pulled up on his computer screen, not knowing what best to do from here. He wished the answer would just pop into his mind, like the glow from that proverbial light bulb, but he'd already second-guessed his second guess.

He supposed he could take his conundrum to Mr. Stetson, but he'd just hate to have to do that. He didn't want to come off as incompetent, much less around his boss, but if anyone could give him the official yay or nay on his trouble, it would surely be Mr. Stetson. Besides, it was like his mother always said: "better safe than sorry." And if he'd learned anything from working with life insurance, it was *far* better to be safe than it was to be sorry. They were dealing with people's money, after all, and that came with an awful lot of responsibility. And such responsibility shouldn't be forgone just because he was feeling like a Nervous Nelly.

He clicked the printer symbol on his troublesome form and then locked his computer screen, just like his cyber security courses had always stressed when leaving one's desk. He rose from his chair and tugged his vest down, making sure he looked proper and smart. Then he headed out of his cubicle, reminding himself to do exactly what the kitten on his wall-calendar said: "Hang in there!"

The office was pretty quiet today, most people sticking to their desks and staying focused on their tasks rather than milling around, chatting with each other about their weekends, sports, or the latest gossip. It was usually a bit more upbeat than this, but Paul just figured that his co-workers were going through some extra-tough cases of the Mondays.

Daniel Hawkins must've been having a *really* bad go of it, because when Paul passed his desk, he didn't pop out and razz him about his attire. Daniel seemed to have a radar sense for whenever Paul came around to the printer, and he always had some rib-tickler to share about Paul's choice of clothing; but Daniel didn't even so much as turn around when Paul grabbed his copy of the change form. And here Paul had expected a real good zinger about his brand new Bill Nye tube socks.

He shrugged the matter off; maybe he'd print something else later on and give Daniel another opportunity.

Paul turned back about, heading for Mr. Stetson's office on the opposite side of the building. The theme song to *Gilligan's Island* randomly popped into his head as he strode down the aisles of cubicles, as it had a nasty habit of doing, but he indulged it, humming the catchy tune as he went along.

He glanced to his left, looking out a flank of windows and to the wheat fields that sat only yards off from their building. A big old harvester sat out there, still and quiet. The owner must have been having some mechanical troubles with it, because it'd been in the same spot since all of last week. Paul couldn't even begin to imagine how to go about fixing such a beast. He'd never been too good with machines or engines or anything of that sort. Give him a Klotski or an Alexander's Star, and that would be a different story; but if it ran on gas or had wires, well—

Paul was pulled out of his wandering thoughts by the sudden whiff of some pungent odor.

It was so pronounced that it forced him to a stop, the sheer rank of it causing him to shudder all over. It smelled like something had spoiled, like days-old trash or something of the sort. But where could it be coming from?

Paul dared to take a few quick sniffs of the air, angling his nose here and there, trying to get a bead on the source of the foulness.

It seemed like, whatever it was, it was coming from off to his left, around a cubicle where a new hire was sitting, clicking through some screens on his computer. Paul had seen the young man up and about in the last couple weeks, but he didn't know his name, and they didn't have a placard for him to place outside his cube yet.

"Hey there," Paul said, as chipper as he could manage, in light of that reek. "How's it going?"

The young man didn't seem to know he was being addressed, as he didn't turn around or acknowledge Paul in the least.

Not wanting to be rude, but unwilling to go unnoticed, Paul stepped into the young man's cube and gave his plaid-shirted shoulder a tap. "This is Paul Larsen transmitting; is there anybody out there?"

He chuckled at his own joke as the youth finally turned about, slowly revolving in his seat and looking up to Paul through thick glasses that made his eyes seem unnaturally bulbous.

"Pardon my interruption, young sir. Paul's the name and insurance is my game!"

He extended a hand. The young man glanced down at it with a tilt of his head, as though handshakes were an utterly foreign concept to him; he looked back up to Paul, a blank look on his face.

"Well, uhm, I'm pleased to meet you. I was just walking by and, well . . ." Paul thought on how to best put the matter, that smell still making the hairs in his nose tingle. "Pardon my French, but . . . golly! It smells a bit bad over here, don't you think?"

The young man just shrugged and sat there, staring at him, neither blinking nor sparing a word.

"I didn't know if maybe . . . well, I hate to put a mark on our reputation, seeing as how you just started here and all, but we've been known to have some troubles with mice in the building. They like to make little beds for themselves in drawers and get into people's food, and sometimes . . . well, I didn't know if Mickey Mouse had gone off to a greener pasture in one of your drawers!"

The young man staid quiet and still as Paul had another laugh, one that gradually died off under the youth's persistent gaze.

This silent treatment was getting to be a bit too much for Paul. Sure, his co-workers were never all that chatty with him, but this was taking it to another degree.

He gave a shrug of his own and inched back out of the new hire's cube. "Well, just thought I'd mention it to you. I'll leave you to it. Pleased to meet you, and have a good day."

Paul went on his way, the new hire still glancing at him from over his wall. The fellow seemed a tad peculiar, but maybe he was just painfully introverted, especially being the new guy and all. And bad smells weren't exactly the best topic for get-to-know-you talks.

Paul decided he'd try and strike up another conversation with the young man sometime, perhaps if they ran across each other in the break room.

Paul hung a right and then a left, heading down a hall that led to the offices of some of the higher-ups. He stepped up to Mr. Stetson's closed door, fixing his vest again and doing a little mental run-through of what he'd say. When he had it down, he knocked on the door and peeked his head in.

His boss sat behind his desk, hands clasped on his desktop, attention on his computer screen. He was decked out in one of his many fine tweed suits, which Paul had always found to be quite snazzy, no matter what others tended to whisper.

"Excuse me for the intrusion, Mr. Stetson, but I have something here that's been a pain in my behind. Would you happen to have the time to see if you can lend a hand?"

His boss gave a slow grunt of approval, keeping his eyes to his work as Paul stepped up to his desk.

"I have a beneficiary change form here with an electronic signature from the policy owner. Now, I've never known us to accept electronic signatures, but I've been hearing that quality's sending back the rejection letters that processors have been doing, saying we *do* accept them as of the start of this month. I don't believe I ever heard anything about that change in protocol, myself. So, I thought I should hear it from you: do we or don't we take electronic signatures now?"

There was a stretch of silence before Mr. Stetson gave a little grumble that Paul couldn't interpret.

He stepped up closer to his boss, slipping around the side of his desk, taking a glance at what held Mr. Stetson's attention so. But Mr. Stetson's computer screen was a blank black, with nothing across it but his own reflection.

"Sir?" Paul asked after a hesitant second. "Sir, is everything all right?"

Mr. Stetson gave a slight nod, still looking at his screen.

"Ah! I know what it is: Mrs. Stetson made another one of her wonderful Sunday dinners last night, and you're still slobber-knocked by how yummy it was!"

Paul laughed and gave a playful tap on his boss' desk. Mr. Stetson turned about and looked to where Paul had rapped his knuckles, but he still wouldn't look him in the eye.

Paul could sense his visit was going mostly unnoticed, so he cleared his throat and got back to the matter at hand. "So, should I go ahead and process the change, Mr. Stetson?"

His boss blinked and looked back up to his computer screen.

"Yes," he mumbled.

Paul gave a curt nod and sidestepped back over to the office door. "Thanks for your time, Mr. Stetson. Have a fine day, and give my best to the missus!"

Paul paused for a thank you and well-wishing of his own, but he didn't get one. Mr. Stetson had turned his attention to the phone at his elbow, as though patiently expecting it to ring.

Paul looked down at his shoes and slipped back out into the hall, shutting the door behind him with a sigh. At least he had his answer, and now he could get back to work.

***

As Paul Larsen made his way back to his desk, he couldn't help but spare a bitter thought, thinking of how his boss was just plain dead on his derriere today. The terrible irony lay in just how true it was.

Mr. Stetson *was* dead on his derriere, much like everyone else who'd been in the office of Midwest Life since the day of November 12th, 2018, when an enemy of the nation initiated a test run of a newly developed bioweapon in the small town of Rumsford, Tennessee.

The strike had been meticulously planned, statistics garnered and contingencies set in motion long before the implantation of a sleeper agent, who had transported the weapon into the community and acted as its caretaker until the date of execution was decided. Enemy scientists had boldly promised that their creation would bring a mortality rate of one hundred percent upon the unsuspecting town; in reality, the lethal agent had weeded off only ninety-three percent of the total population, leaving 342 citizens alive and terrified in the wake of the attack, fleeing their homes in terror and bringing stories of woe and doom to the neighboring communities they ran to. They spoke of how family and neighbors collapsed all across town that morning, and all within a matter of an hour, convulsing and coughing up blood, choking on bile and screaming in pain. No one place was saved from the onslaught; the agent found its way into schools, the local hospital, churches—everywhere.

In light of the ensuing chaos, the U.S. government enforced a prompt and rigid quarantine the likes of which the country had never known, evacuating whole communities within the vicinity of Rumsford for fear of the bioweapon's spread, containing those who had been present at the time of the attack and closely monitoring the people they'd come into contact with. Analyses and theories were being posited as to what had made survivors immune to the weapon's attack, but a definite conclusion was still weeks off, at best.

Given the mass fatalities—and in hesitance to venture into the town before having a greater understanding of the contagion—the U.S. government held off on sending anyone into the quarantine zone, for any reason. Retrieval of the deceased was out of the immediate question, and the idea of finding any other survivors in the desolation seemed beyond the realm of likelihood; and, even if so, there were other, more pressing matters that needed consideration, namely how to handle the media's response to the event and the looming question of retaliation.

That dreadful attack had occurred a full seven days ago, when—for the first time in his eight years with the company—Paul Larsen called in sick.

While he slept off the worst cold he'd ever had, his co-workers were breathing in the substance that claimed nearly all of their lives, dying in their cubicles and falling in the hallways as the bioweapon forced its way into the air of the building. The agent had been released only a half-mile off from the Midwest Life location, and as such, they were among the first fatalities of the day.

And while the town's survivors fled the area, screaming and crying their fears, Paul woke up to take a long, hot shower, hoping it would make him feel better. And then, after Rumsford had become a silent graveyard, he sat down to a bowl of chicken-noodle soup, sitting in the lonesome stillness of his measly apartment and working on a puzzle he'd started the day before.

When he woke the next morning and made his way to work, he thought that maybe he was still in his bed, fast asleep. All the people lying about and all the cars abandoned on the road—it sure seemed like something from a dream. A bad dream. Telling himself that that's what it had to be, he finished driving to work, and when he walked into the building, he stopped and took the carnage in, wishing that the dream would end.

Seeing the blood that Mary Fallon had hacked up on her computer, stepping over Dean Withers in the break room—it was all so terrible. Too terrible to comprehend.

Too terrible to be real.

And so, his mind allowed him to think that it wasn't.

It was easy enough to do, after a few gallons of tears were shed and a few strands of hair were pulled from his head. And after he'd gone around the building, putting people back in their cubicles and helping them tidy up their dropped papers, the scene was effectively set. Some madness may have set in, but oddly enough, it lit the light that led him back to normalcy. And since his co-workers rarely spoke to him when they *were* alive, and since he often had to do others' work for them, anyway, things were—in a sense—very much like they had been before.

And for Paul, that was just fine.

It was just another Monday.

The Puckwudgie, or Thomas Clay and His Convictions

1644

The night was growing cold, but the fire—meager as it was—did its task in keeping the October chill at bay. It was only when a breeze came wafting out from the nearby harbor and through the bared trees of Winter Island that Cuthbert Blake and Thomas Clay felt perturbed enough to scoot their log seats closer to the kindling, hunching their shoulders at the rush of air and shifting their rifles from one shoulder to the other. The seaside gust brought the thick smell of brine and fish into the fort; while the wooden walls of the fortification had long since been permeated and filled with the reek, the men stationed there hardly ever noticed, their nostrils having grown quite accustomed—save for when those harsh breezes came in.

"Guh!" Blake groaned, pulling a hand from the fire and holding its back to his nose. "When God made the sea, he made it wondrous, indeed; but could he not have thought a better smell for it?"

Clay, the younger of the two (with hardly a hair sprouting from his thin chin) and by far the firmer in their faith, turned his eyes from the flames and focused them upon the other private. He held a cautious finger out to his compatriot, as a vicar would before a child approaching the brink of blasphemy. His words held all the certainty of the ancient wise—or just the very young. "The Lord made it as he saw fit, Blake, and your scoundrel's nose is no apt judge of His makings."

Blake gave a good laugh at this. "A funny thing; my wife said the same to me of her cooking!" The man gave his knee a proud smack as he chuckled on, and in spite of himself, Clay joined in.

It felt good to have some degree of merriment, if only it were this little joke. While their duty as guards was not in itself a very laborious task, as soldiers, Clay had often prescribed to the stalwart and alert disposition his training had fought to enforce in him and his compatriots. He took to it easily, something he'd likened and attributed to his steadfastness in faith; it was easier, he thought, to be a soldier for country when one was already a soldier for God. And this was indeed what he'd come to fancy himself as, a warrior bearing the teachings of his Lord, side by side with an army of the righteous Puritans, who may yet provide conquest over those faiths that did not tread the one true path.

As though to remind him of the need for constancy, their superior, Captain Joseph Harding, came round the corner in that moment, instantly silencing Clay and Blake as they stood at attention.

"At ease, men," Harding said with a wave of his gloved hand. "Though be not too eased."

Taking the captain's words as a critique, Blake spoke up to save face and give excuse, though in a dutiful tone. "All is well about the fort tonight, Captain. Neither a sight nor sound out of place."

"Very good," the captain nodded. Though there was a certain sternness to his face that was not usually there. And the way his sight was drawn to the wall of the fortification was somehow odd; his eyes lingered there, as though he were not looking to the wall itself, but to something beyond it that only he could see, out in the night about them. As young Clay looked upon him, studying him, he realized it was not, in fact, sternness, but some level of worry on his commander's bearded features. Harding, it seemed, was apprehensive about something.

"Is there something the matter, sir?"

The captain kept his eye upon the wall a moment longer. Then he turned back around, eyes downcast. "No, young Clay. Nothing I can rightly put words to, at the least."

"I'm sorry, sir?" Clay inquired. It was very unlike the captain to be so distracted, and by seemingly nothing.

Harding shook his head. "Just a feeling, lad. A notion that will not leave my head. All I ask is that you keep a keen eye on matters this night."

"For what, sir?" Blake put in. He, too, was curious as to what the captain was on about.

Harding gave a sigh, another shake of his head, and shrugged. "I've worries that may be quite unfounded, but I believe you should be wary of the forests tonight."

Clay clutched his rifle more tightly. "What is it, sir? Do you fear that there may be savages about tonight?"

The captain frowned and shook his head again. "No. Just that strange things may be wanton to occur. It is All Hallow's Eve, this night. It is a time for praying to and recognizing our many saints, but it is also a time when—I fear—the veils between worlds are thin. When things far older than men may tread the land more bravely . . ."

At this, Clay felt a swell of proud anger rise up in his chest. Here his commander had instilled caution in him, and for nothing more than impossible and superstitious babble.

"Then rest well, Captain," the youth said, easing back onto his log. "For no such things exists. In this land or any other. Man reigns upon earth, and God reigns over earth. He would not see such things to be." That he should even need to say such a thing to a fellow Puritan—and his superior, nonetheless—boggled young Clay's mind.

The captain turned around and focused a steady gaze upon his subordinates—Clay, in particular.

""There are more things in heaven and earth," or so it has been said. Steady Puritan foot has not tread upon this land for more than twenty years, Thomas; it is far too short a time for the civilized to learn the extent of its cunning, and for it to reveal its many secrets. Besides, I myself have . . . seen things . . . since the colonies were founded. Had experiences I cannot rightly stand to reason. Why, it was on this very eve two years ago—on watch, just like you men— that I witnessed some peculiar luminescence hanging about within those trees just beyond our fortification."

Harding took a step closer towards the wall, a step into the memory of his so-called experience, remembering. "It was a cold night then, as well. I was growing weary, but I would not turn my eyes from the woods. It was so very dark then, and it had me quite on edge. Then, out of the chilled air, this wisp of blue-gray light appeared amidst the bramble of the trees! It had the form of a torch's flame, dancing and licking as fire, but it swayed as though it were . . . alive!"

The captain turned back around, the truth (or, at least, his *believed* truth) of the matter in his eyes. "It hovered about for a fair moment. Long enough for me to question my sight and sanity. And then it moved off into the woods, as though carried by the breeze, disappearing and tempting me to follow after it. I knew not what it could be and the knowledge still escapes me. But I swear to the heavens that I did truly see it, and that it was of a nature beyond the natural realm. I've not seen its like since, but still, I remember. And I am cautious."

In spite of his rank, Clay brandished a harsh and judging look upon his captain once the latter had fallen silent.

""When you come into the land that the Lord your God is giving you, you shall not learn to follow the abominable practices of those nations." Captain, you speak of such things as only those savages beyond our walls would; it's their ilk who believes in ghosts and goblins and those heathen creatures of the night, and of children's imaginations. It is ours to believe in God and his way of the world."

Harding regarded the lad with a weary smile. "You've the fortitude of faith, my boy. Most admirable. But you've little in the ways of experience, and once you've gained it, you may well find there are a fair number of things in this world you had never even conceived of."

The captain turned away from them then, the debate over and his say passed. He trudged off, going back towards the barracks. "Have a good night, gentlemen, and stay alert."

Clay could not help but shoot a sneer at the captain's back as he turned a corner. As soon as he was out of sight, Blake gave his comrade a playful tap on the shoulder.

"I always thought our captain was quite the admirer of English manufacture, but it seems he's been drinking it for a good time, now!"

Blake let loose a hearty laugh, but Clay did not join in this time. He merely sat there, putting his hands back to the fire and stewing over the captain's Banbury tale.

***

The hour was late and the moon was out in full now, the evening's clouds having departed and opened up to the starry firmament. It was a dazzling sight, no doubt, but Thomas Clay would have readily traded it for a cot and a pillow.

He was alone now, walking about his post while Blake sauntered about somewhere on the opposite side of the fort. He'd grown to miss the heat of their fire, the air having grown more frigid as midnight marched their way. His feet ached ever so slightly, but he would not allow himself to rest a spell. His duty was his duty, and it was as simple as that.

He'd not bothered to think any more on his commander's superstitious assertions in the hours that had since passed. His convictions would not deign to entertain such drivel any longer. Instead, he turned his searching eyes out to the woods, peering through the slats between the beams of oak that made up the fort's wall.

All was still out there. The trees and bushes were covered by a very thin frost, as was the grass. It discolored their dead and dying limbs with a hint of white, the blades of the grass looking as though they bore a rather pitiful snowfall. He could not see very far into the forest, despite the bright moon overhead; the trees grew too closely over here to glimpse much further than twenty feet away.

Still, that fact did not stop him from seeing a small, darting form that was suddenly making its way along the tree line.

At first, young Clay thought it to be merely a trick of the light, just a thin tree swaying in the breeze and begging his eye. But there was no breeze, and the subtle snapping of twigs—as though breaking under some foot—made the soldier think otherwise. Stopping his pacing, Clay slid up to the wall and angled himself to where he had a good view out at the bordering forest.

He saw it again, the motion of something—no, some*one*—moving among the trees, slowly walking from the pines just before Clay's eyes and off towards the right. As he narrowed his sight, he thought he could discern . . . a leg! Yes—a short, bared leg, without a single garment upon it. Then he saw an arm, a tiny hand at its end grabbing hold of a tree trunk as the wandering figure made its way through the trees. Finally, he thought he spied a wild length of dark hair hanging about a face he simply couldn't make out.

Why, with a leg so short and a hand so small, it must have been a child! Yes, and no more than a babe, judging by the diminutive form which Clay believed he saw.

"Child!" he called out! "What are you doing out there?!"

His surprise, though great, was trumped by his concern. If that was, indeed, a child out there—and a naked one, at that—then it was in danger of freezing to death in the frost of the evening. But what would a child be doing out here? Surely it could not be from the town, and it wasn't likely to belong to the natives, either. And yet . . .

The figure, seemingly deaf to his comment, kept walking along, and then disappeared into the woods and away from the fort.

"A child!" Clay shouted back to the barracks, to anyone who might hear the report. "There is a child outside the walls!"

Not waiting for an answer to his call, he bolted over to the nearest gates of the fort, unlatching the doors and thrusting one open as he ran outside. Fearing that the child would lose itself to the forest, he gave chase, his rifle still in hand and his feet carrying him swiftly.

He kept calling as he went, looking frantically about for the babe. Though it couldn't have gone very far, it was nowhere in sight.

His fear rising, he dashed along, uncertain of how far he'd gone, though when he'd spared a glance back to see if others were on the hunt, the fort was not in sight. Still, he chased on, going deeper into the woods—until he skidded to a halt.

The child was sitting atop a fallen and rotting pine, its naked back to him. Its shaggy head was hunkered low and its arms bent in, hands up to its face.

Clay heard the tearing and chewing of meat as the babe gave a shake of its head.

"Child?" he prodded, bringing his rifle down.

The babe whirled about—but it was no child, at all.

A big-nosed, needle-toothed creature faced him, snarling wildly, with blood sleeked across its mouth and tongue. A bit of fur-covered flesh hung from its pointed chin. Its hands—much larger than Clay had assumed, nearly bigger than a grown man's—held a crushed squirrel, a red gap torn out of its small chest.

The thing gave a shrill wail, stirring Clay to scream, as well, and to raise his rifle to the beast.

Before he could squeeze off his lone shot, an arrow came whizzing by, its tip driving into the bark of the tree to his left. Another immediately came down into the soil before his foot, this one's tip aflame.

Clay looked ahead again, mouth agape as he saw a half dozen other of the short, nude creatures emerging from the trees, small bows and arrows strung and at the ready. They rushed towards him, their big feet smacking the cold earth as they drew back their bows.

Clay fired in a hurry, the rifle going off with a puff of smoke and a wallop. The shot went wide, missing one of the creatures by a few feet.

Going wild at the blare of the gun, the creatures started hopping up and down in a frenzy, chittering and whooping before loosing their arrows at him. Flaming arches sailed by Clay's head as he stumbled backwards, holding an arm up to try and guard himself from their attack. Each arrow missed him, save for one that went straight into the meat of his calf. Clay screamed in agony as its fiery tip seared his flesh. On instinct, he grabbed the foot-and-a-half long shaft and tore it free from his leg, dropping the smoking arrow to the ground.

The terrified man turned and ran off—or scooted along as best as he could, that was; his wounded leg refused to bend and move properly, each step sending a flare of pain all along the limb. He moaned with each rush of breath, the chilly air fogging up before his numbed face.

More arrows followed, and he could hear the small men giving chase right behind him. He prayed to God for strength and speed, or that He might smite these devilish things with His fury. Above all, he prayed to live, that he might see the light of the morrow.

He hadn't made it more than a dozen yards when he felt the skin of his back cutting open, and then the horrid burn that followed quickly after.

With tears in his eyes, Clay fell to the earth, kicking up dirt and dead leaves as he rolled onto his back. The arrow lodged in his shoulder snapped against the earth as he turned about, delivering another rush of pain. But he had little time to pay it any mind; his gaze went up to the trees, where he saw another of the horrible beasts perched on a branch, its bow pulled back and its flaming arrow aimed right for him.

The creature let it fly with an angry grunt; Clay hadn't even the time to yell in terror before the arrow went through his left eye. The burning of it went unfelt, for he died in that very instant.

Clay's body fell back into the earth, his one remaining eye looking blankly up to the heaven that would accept him.

***

The soldiers of the fort found their missing comrade nearly an hour later, his skin pale with his death and the state of his eye making the steeliest of them shudder.

A handful had heard Thomas Clay's shout and followed after him, after quickly dressing and grabbing their weapons. Captain Harding had led the charge, Cuthbert Blake right beside him. But by then, the young soldier was too far ahead of them, and they knew not where along the tree line he'd run off to. They'd been searching in all that time, and now that they'd found him, they looked nervously to the woods about them.

"Savages did this!" Blake had spat, his rifle tightly gripped and scanning the darkness. "That blasted arrow proves it!"

Captain Harding would have been inclined to agree, were it not for the strange size of the arrow. It was peculiar, and far too short to belong to any of the tribe's he was aware of. And yet, upon further inspection, they found a few scattered prints of grown men's bare feet pressed into the soil, and there was no other soul or group in this land who would be likely to kill in such a manner.

All Harding had known for sure was that he needed to return his men to the safety of their station, and to gather up the dead lad's body for a Christian burial on the morrow. Giving his orders, two men carried poor Thomas Clay while the rest kept their sights upon the trees, waiting for another attack.

None came. The forests had grown quiet again, the darkness hiding whoever—or whatever—may have called them home.

Her Name's Not John

Dean Andrews swayed back and forth in the elevator of his apartment complex. His motion was more from the effects of one too many Bud Lights than a compulsion to dance to the bland elevator music playing in the lift. The low, melodic ditty did little for the nausea he was just barely holding back. A night of drinking with his buddies at Tony D's Bar and Grill had supplied the alcohol, as well as the tacos now churning in Dean's stomach. The tacos of Taco Tuesday were always cheaply made, but tasted oddly phenomenal the more one drank. Dean had drank plenty and eaten plenty.

As the doors of the elevator opened, he rushed out and down to his apartment, a hand over his mouth. The tacos weren't going to last long.

Dean stumbled over his feet as the elevator doors shut behind him. He lurched forward, fighting the buzz and trying to keep his balance. He managed to keep his footing and keep the rolling contents of his stomach in their place for another moment. Reaching his free hand into his pocket, he grabbed his keys and stepped up to his apartment door. The jangling keys were a clamor in the midnight silence of the hallway, but Dean didn't care. He only cared if he could make it to the bathroom in time for the purge.

The aftertaste of beef and lettuce was coming up his throat as he slipped into his apartment. The bathroom was only a few feet away, but the perspiration and heat under his collar made it seem like a marathon run. He made it just in time.

The lid of the toilet was up—blessedly so. He took enough time to flick on the light (just so he could see well enough to aim), tossed his keys to the floor, and knelt down over the toilet. He hurled, the sound of his retching echoing against the inside of the toilet bowl.

Dean was glad Christine wasn't here to see this—his head in the toilet and his drinking days nowhere near behind him. She'd dropped her partying ways immediately after college; Dean's had only increased. They'd had some crazy times at some crazy parties in their college years, but graduation had made Christine dry almost automatically, resolute in her ways to never again drink a drop. The prospect of "real life" had made her serious and level-headed, but she wasn't a prude about his continued alcoholic endeavors—though, sometimes, Dean thought otherwise. She knew of his drinking binges with his work buddies, condoning it only to a degree. But if she saw him now, she'd probably kick his ass to the curb in pure revulsion. Three years spent together would go down the toilet like the muck of his stomach now making its way out of him.

His midsection slowly eased itself, and he spit out the dreadful taste in his mouth. Pushing himself back, Dean sat his back against the side of the tub and sat down, legs sprawled outwards. He wiped a hand over his head and neck, flicking off the sweat. His breathing slowed to a settled rhythm. A sudden gurgle from within leapt up, though, and he got back to his knees and threw up, bracing his hands against the tank of the toilet.

In between his choked purging, he heard a voice speaking up. "Oh, poor baby . . ."

Dean felt a surge of shame and worry shoot through him.

He pictured Christine standing in the doorway of the bathroom, a surprise nightly visit in her mind. Her voice was soothing, a smooth, sympathetic tone in her cadence. He knew that caring voice would be replaced by an angry glare and measured silence the moment he looked up at her and she realized his sickness was a product of his care-free drinking rather than a more natural ailment.

Swallowing down his worry (and a bit more), he pulled his head out of the porcelain.

"Hey, babe," he whispered, his throat raw and sensitive. Turning his head to the doorway, he tried to put on his most pitiful puppy-dog stare to ease Christine's inevitable disappointment.

The innocent facade faded as he realized Christine wasn't there. No one was there. The bathroom was empty save for him.

"The hell . . .?" Dean whispered to himself. He knew he'd heard the voice. It was distinctly female. "Someone there?" he called, his voice scratching its way out.

"Right here, baby."

The voice came as clear and as close as if it were spoken from within the bathroom. Still, there was no one else there but Dean. Nevertheless, the calming and feminine voice spoke up again.

"You okay, hun?"

Dean listened closely as the words came. He looked to the toilet before him, the white porcelain glinting in the light from above the sink.

The voice was coming from the toilet. The toilet itself was speaking to him.

He started laughing.

He couldn't help but chuckle, no matter how much it irritated his scratchy throat. He had to be way more drunk than he'd given himself credit for, after all. When toilets spoke to you, you weren't just buzzed, you were flying.

Sure, he'd had some strange times in his drunken hazes—who didn't? He'd streaked down Main Street once back in college, a piccolo in one hand and a Big Mac in the other; he'd French-kissed a Doberman and had a photograph taken by a friend to prove it; he'd even had a one-sided, hour long conversation with one of his shirts his dazed senses had mistaken for Christine. But this was the first time an inanimate object had spoken back. He found it to be oddly hilarious.

"Talking to a toilet you just threw up in brings a whole new meaning to being shit-faced," he said, giggling as his stomach finally eased into normality.

Light, pleasant laughter came from the toilet, mingling with Dean's. It sounded very happy. He now realized it was coming from the lip of the rim, issuing outwards from the bowl that still held his vomit.

"Feeling better?" the toilet asked. It sounded flirtatious and concerned at the same time. Its voice was like that of a young woman's, perhaps twenty or a little older, girlish in its exaggerated tone, yet mature in its almost sensual care.

Dean shook his head at the absurdity of the situation. Despite the ridiculousness of talking to a toilet, he kept the conversation going.

"Yeah. Yeah, I'm feeling a lot better, actually."

And he was. And it wasn't just from the relief of purging the alcohol and the tacos that played hell on his stomach. He felt better talking with his toilet. The voice and its lilt calmed his nerves, caused the slight tremor of his intoxicated limbs to still. Made him feel understood. Made him feel cared for. Made him feel loved.

"Good, glad to hear it," the porcelain said. If it had a face, it sounded like it would be smiling wide.

Dean lifted a hand to the silver handle of the tank and pulled it down. "Fire in the hole!" he said boisterously, feeling his buzz taking over once more. Laughter came from the rim of the toilet again and the water and vomit in the toilet swirled and disappeared.

"Now you go get some sleep, funny man," Dean's porcelain friend said sweetly. "I'll see you in the morning."

Dean nodded at the toilet and rubbed his hand over the cool, smooth outside of the bowl. Its chilled, round surface felt good against the warmth of his hand. He patted it appreciatively, lovingly. He'd often done the same kind of thing to Christine whenever they were together, arm draped around her, stroking the small of her back.

Dean stood up, pushing himself to his feet with help from the edge of the bathtub and grabbing his keys from the floor. He checked himself to see if any flecks from his retching were on his shirt and jeans. Satisfied that there weren't any half-digested remains, he began making his way out of the bathroom. He continued to sway uncertainly, the alcohol he'd consumed still in his system.

As he flicked off the light, the toilet spoke up again.

"Good night." The words were said with a tender appreciation that made him smile.

Dean waved at the toilet and said his thanks. He turned out into the hall, made his way to the bedroom, and fell into his bed.

He slept.

***

The morning brought a hangover, a headache, and the urge to urinate. Each made Dean forget about his late-night conversation with his toilet.

Still in his clothes from the day before, Dean worked his way out of bed and trudged to the bathroom. He bumped a shoulder into the wall, his equilibrium still for squat. The pain that shot through his arm only barely registered, compared to every other sensation fighting to taking precedence. His bladder was straining and his hangover was taking a jackhammer to his brain.

He flicked the light on in the bathroom, instantly regretting it; the light made his eyes throb. Squinting, he walked over to the toilet, unbuckling his belt and unzipping his fly.

"Oh, my," a sultry voice said. "Is that for me?"

Dean stopped in mid-stream. Literally. He looked down at the toilet, struggling to place the sense of Déjà vu that swept over him. Then he remembered the previous night: the drinking, the vomiting, and the voice.

His toilet was speaking to him once again. Which was odd, especially because he wasn't drunk now, just hung over. This left Dean at a loss. Conversing with a toilet may be fun when you're inebriated, but doing so when you were sobering up was pushing it. It was the kind of thing people in straight-jackets did.

But, still, that smooth, feminine voice was hard to deny. Finally, he answered.

"Uh . . . yeah . . ."

"Well, go ahead. Don't let me stop you," the toilet said, letting out a playful little laugh. "Give it to me, big fella."

Dean swallowed down hard, wondering briefly if he was losing it. He wondered what it would feel like to wear a straight-jacket, himself. Deciding he didn't like that idea, he chalked this experience up to the remnants of one hell of a binge, and nothing more—or so he hoped.

He pushed on with his deed, trying to look anywhere but the toilet. As he whizzed, he heard the voice from the toilet give a pleasurable hum.

"*Mmmhhmm . . .*"

Dean couldn't help it. He felt the urge to say what was on his mind.

"You keep doing that, and you're going to make me feel like R-Kelly."

He zipped his fly and reached for the handle. The toilet laughed again, sounding genuinely pleased. "Thanks for the input, you joker," she said. "Much appreciated."

The water in the bowl swirled down, and the noise of it covered more laughter—coming from both Dean and his toilet.

Dean turned around, perplexed as to what to do or say next. He rubbed a hand over the back of his head, shrugged, and waved at his toilet. A nervous chuckle escaped him. "Well, uh . . . see you later."

"You can count on it, fella," she said. *She*? When, exactly, did he start thinking of his toilet as a she rather than an it?

Dean turned off the light and went into the kitchen, pondering. He popped open a container of Excedrin and chewed down two pills, hoping it would clear his head and make things straight. While he stood there, chewing and thinking, his cell phone rang in his back pocket. His ringtone sent a pang through his skull, and he fished it out and answered it quickly.

"Hello?" he said, trying to mask the discomfort in his voice in case it was Christine. It was.

"Hey, tiger," she said, sounding cheery and blissfully sober. "You weren't hanging from any chandeliers last night with your boys, were you?" There was good humor in the question, but Dean picked up on something more to it. Some ridicule. He didn't care for it, but he put on a smile as he answered.

"No, no," he said quickly—perhaps too quickly. "Just a couple rounds."

Christine laughed on the other end, sounding like she accepted his lie. "Good," she said, "because I was hoping you'd come over to my place tonight and we could hang out. And I want you cheerful and present. Maybe we can fool around a little, too."

Dean sighed, pulling the phone back so Christine couldn't hear it. He couldn't say no, but he sure hoped he could shake the hangover before tonight came.

"Yeah," he answered, trying to sound as excited as possible. "The usual time? Six o'clock?"

"Yep," Christine agreed. "I'll see you then, tiger. Love you."

"Love you, too," Dean said, and he ended the call before she could say anything else. He opened the container of Excedrin again and swallowed two more pills. He'd need them.

***

Six o'clock came and a few hours of watching television and chatting about each other's lives followed.

Dean had managed to reduce his hangover to a bearable ache. Three goes at brushing his teeth blocked any leftover smell of regurgitated tacos or loads of beer. He put on plenty of cologne to hide that he hadn't showered. Showering wasn't something he felt entirely safe doing, because he didn't want to risk chatting with his toilet again, pleasant voice or no.

Christine had spent the evening snuggled up against Dean on her couch, talking all the while and trying to get him to join in. But he remained quiet throughout her questions and the shows they watched; his mind was too busy trying to wrap itself around the conundrum of his talking toilet.

He sure as hell wouldn't tell Christine about it. She'd accuse him of being a true alcoholic, "dependent" and all other manner of negative terms being thrust on him. If not that, she'd probably call him crazy. Which he wondered more and more about, himself.

When a *Daily Show* rerun had gone to commercial, he excused himself to use Christine's bathroom. She gave him a lusty look as he left, asking him to make it quick.

He entered her bathroom slowly, staring at the toilet with frazzled nerves. He braced himself for another outspoken piece of toiletry, stepped up to it, and went about his business. But as he urinated, no voice came from Christine's bathroom; no words of conversation rang out from her toilet, no laughter, no soothing cadence. Dean was surprised to realize that this disappointed him, in a way. He'd liked how his own toilet had spoken to him, how it truly seemed to appreciate and enjoy his company. He wondered if his toilet would speak to him again when he returned and now that he was sober. As he wondered, he began to hope.

Dean walked back into Christine's living room, a hand over his stomach, as if it were troubling him.

"Hey, babe," he said, trying to sound like he was in pain. "I'm not feeling all that well. I think I might be catching something."

Christine's lustful look faded into automatic concern. It should have made Dean feel guilty for lying, but it really didn't.

"Oh, poor baby!" she said, standing up from the couch. Her concern seemed a little less genuine to him than in the past. Not nearly as worried as his toilet had sounded. He waved her off, making sure she wouldn't come near him.

"I'm going to just go home and try to sleep it off. If you don't mind, of course."

She closed the distance between them despite his motions, nodding as they both reached the door. She wrapped her arms around his neck and hugged him, kissing his cheek. "Of course, sweetie," she said. "You get to feeling better. We'll pick up where we left off later on."

She shot him a smile that was meant to be sexy, but Dean didn't see it. He said his goodbyes and was out the door as quick as he could manage.

He drove back to his apartment in a rush. The elevator was too slow going up. He got off the lift and practically ran to his apartment, rushing inside. He walked into the bathroom and looked expectantly at the toilet.

"There you are," the sweet feminine voice said. It sounded glad to see him again. "You got something for me?"

Dean, overjoyed to hear the voice again, nodded and moved to stand over the toilet. "You bet I do," he grunted. His hands moved to his zipper, undoing his pants and letting them fall to his ankles. He grabbed hold of himself and began stroking.

The toilet egged him on, providing words of encouragement and longing, turning him on all the more. It made him feel ashamed, too; guilty, like he was cheating, betraying Christine by being with another. He kind of liked it. Besides, could you really cheat on a partner with an inanimate object? The feeling of doing something forbidden mixed with his swelling satisfaction, heating his skin and sending it into a burning wave of sensation. Finally, he released himself in a moan of pleasure. The mouth of the toilet accepted it and the voice giggled in joy.

"Thanks, big fella," the toilet said. Dean gave his own thanks.

He pulled up his pants, buckling them back up, and then sat down on the bathroom floor. Leaning his head against the bathtub, he began talking with the toilet, telling it about his life, his troubles, and his pleasures.

The toilet listened gratefully.

She was there for him; for his needs, his wants—and his alone.

***

There were points in Dean's life—dull, uneventful, spur-of-the-moment moments—where he passed the time wondering about ultimately useless facts about life. He now recalled wondering on a number of occasions why bathrooms were referred to as "Johns." It had something to do with old times in old England, he thought. Now that he was on speaking terms with a toilet, he thought he'd ask an expert.

"My name's not John," his toilet had answered. "It's Amelia."

Amelia. Dean liked that name. It was rare to hear these days. It had beauty and character.

He thought it was an even prettier name than Christine.

***

Over the next week, Dean and Amelia had numerous conversations together.

His worries of going insane drifted off; he just didn't care. He began drinking all the liquids he could find or chow down on all the food in his fridge just to justify a visit with Amelia. Very quickly, however, he began to go to the bathroom simply to chat with her.

When he wasn't at work or obliging Christine with a date-night, he was in his bathroom, sitting in or beside the tub, Amelia beside him. They spoke like old friends, going into intimate details about each other's lives, mostly about Dean's. He would tell her about how his day went, his job, and his hobbies. Amelia listened respectfully and gave her input when he asked for it and her support when she felt he needed it. Especially when it came to matters of Christine.

Dean didn't realize it at first, but he was telling Amelia of all his dissatisfactions with their relationship—three years' worth of matters he'd thought over before, but never dared to give *too much* thought to. He was venting his frustrations about Christine's straight-edge habits as compared to his devil-may-care drinking, along with his beliefs of how she wanted to change him and have a leash on him with all these date-nights and phone calls she made lately. Amelia agreed that Christine sounded very controlling and judgmental, saying Dean was a great guy and deserved far better than that.

At one point, Amelia blatantly told him: "You should dump her."

Dean, in spite of his many complaints, shrugged it off with a joke. "Dump? Is that toilet humor?"

Amelia had laughed and let the subject go, but Dean would continue to think about it often—leaving Christine and calling it quits. It sounded like a possibility, but he just wasn't sure. He kept on with his criticisms of her, though, giving Amelia more and more of his innermost thoughts and feelings that he never dared to share with Christine.

"I don't judge you, Dean," Amelia constantly said. "I accept you for who you are. And I take care of you, don't I?"

And Dean would always say back: "Yes, Amelia, you do."

She truly did. She was always there for him, helping him to relieve himself, both physically and emotionally.

He began to love her for it.

***

Dean was truly surprised by a surprise visit from Christine one Saturday evening. She arrived at his door with Chinese take-out in hand and a smile on her face.

"Hey, babe," she said as he held the door open, scooting her way into his apartment. "I thought we could have a night to ourselves. I called you a few times earlier, but I guess your phone was off. I took the initiative and just decided to stop by. Hope that's okay. I brought General Tao's!"

Christine made her way into the kitchen while Dean stood there at his door, a little taken aback by her appearance. He knew she had been calling him—he had tried his best to ignore it. And it was more than a few calls—more like seven or eight. Sighing, he shut the door and made his way to the kitchen.

As he passed the bathroom, he reached in and shut the door so Amelia couldn't hear them. He didn't want her to realize that Christine was there, if she didn't know already, and didn't want her to become disappointed in him for not asserting himself and refusing his girlfriend at the door, if that's what he felt like doing.

He walked into the kitchen, fumbling in his mind for a way to end the impromptu visit as quickly as possible. He was coming up with nothing. Christine, in the meantime, was arranging the boxes of takeout on the countertop. She gave him a quick smile and then moved to the cabinets for plates.

"Hey," she said, her back to Dean. "How about you put on some music? Something a little soft, to get the mood going?"

Dean felt a retort threatening to burst out of him. He didn't appreciate Christine just inviting herself over like this and going through his cabinets and dishing out demands. Instead, he just silently walked out of the kitchen, trudging along, feeling more and more like a well-trained puppy at its master's whim.

He crossed the hall and entered the living room, walking to the stereo, perched on a shelf lined with CDs. He began thumbing through his collection, looking for something that could qualify as "soft." Each title of each band he looked over didn't quite fit the bill. Dropkick Murphys, Senses Fail, AC/DC—nope, nope, and no. His fingers flicked through another row of CDs well before he realized that none of them belonged to him. Kanye West, Michael Bublé, and the sort. Christine's music. Music which she had left in his apartment, which she had set here next to his own. Grumbling, he picked up Bublé and took the disc out, inserting it into the stereo port and hitting play. He flinched as overtly melodic piano playing filled the apartment.

Dean ground his teeth and walked back into the kitchen. He started to say something about Christine's music on his shelf, but he stopped short when he looked up. Christine wasn't to be seen at the counter, the table, or the sink. Confused, Dean called out for her. Over the music in the living room, he heard Christine's muffled shout ring out a second later.

"Nature called, tiger!"

Dean felt heat rising under his collar as it dawned on him. Christine was in the bathroom. With Amelia.

Clenching his fists, he moved towards the bathroom, his feet thumping across the floor of his apartment. When the bathroom came into sight, he saw the door was shut, with his nosy girlfriend behind it, using his Amelia. The thought made his nostrils flare and his blood boil. As he reached the door, he twisted the knob and thrust it open.

Christine looked up and over to him, obviously shocked. She sat on his sweet Amelia, her skinny jeans and panties at her ankles. She covered herself on instinct and shot Dean an angry glare.

"Dean, what the hell are—?"

She was cut off as Dean moved to stand right beside her, a precious few feet between them now. "Get off of her," he said coldly.

Perplexed and embarrassed, Christine stumbled over her response. "You . . . I . . . what . . . ?"

Her words became a scream as Dean grabbed a hold of her hair and hauled her upwards. She grabbed at his arm, trying but failing to get free of the grip.

"I said, get off of her!"

Dean tugged Christine up to her feet and then pulled her to the doorway of the bathroom. She stumbled about, her jeans still around her ankles, trying desperately to walk so her hair wasn't uprooted. He tossed her out, pushing her head with all his force, watching as she tumbled forward and out into the hall. She gave a holler, more out of shock and sorrow than pain, landing on all fours.

Dean turned his back to Amelia, moving slowly backwards to guard his toilet. He made no other moves and said nothing more, just glared hatefully at Christine and waited.

Christine had looked his way to see if he would continue the assault. Seeing that he wouldn't, she stood up on her quivering legs. With tears leaking from her eyes in rivers of running mascara, she pulled her panties and her pants back on. Her face—one that he'd once found gorgeous, and which was now just irritating to look at—ran a swath of emotions in a matter of pained seconds. Numbed shock gave way to mounting sorrow and hurt, sorrow and hurt to pure outrage.

In between her choked sobs, she cursed him. "You bastard . . . What's wrong with you, you crazy bastard?! Get away from me!"

She turned to the kitchen and disappeared from Dean's sight. When she came back, her purse was in one hand and her car keys in the other. She only stayed in sight long enough to shout one more thing at him:

"Fucking asshole!"

With that, she turned away to the front door. Still sobbing up a storm, she left, slamming the door shut behind her. Dean was left alone in his apartment, the sound of Michael Bublé the only noise to be heard. But then he remembered he wasn't alone.

"My hero," Amelia said, her voice laced with gratitude and awe. She gave a little laugh that made Dean's anger subside a little. "You finally stood up to the bitch."

Dean swallowed hard and nodded, turning to face Amelia. "I couldn't let her do that to you," he said, his voice trembling from the adrenaline still rushing through him. "I . . . I love you . . ."

Amelia was quiet, but then she whispered, oh-so-sweetly: "I love you too, Dean."

Dean felt a tear of relief and joy drop from his eye. He smiled and knelt down, setting his hands over Amelia's chilled, porcelain exterior. He rubbed and traced her form with a lover's caress, trying to show his passion as best he could. He lifted his head up and kissed her tank repeatedly; he jostled her lever playfully, passionately.

He wondered if Christine would call the cops on him, maybe report him and have him thrown in jail. But he only wondered about this for a moment. Right now, all he knew for sure was that his Amelia loved him, and he loved her, in turn. He laid his head down on her tank and wrapped his arms around her, hugging her tightly as she spoke up again.

"I take care of you, and you take care of me. And that's all we'll ever need, baby."

And this was all that Dean could ever want.

Though He Walks

For as long as he could remember, Nathan Halston had been praying for God to show Himself—somehow, someway. Once the world had fallen to the plague of the Turned, he'd prayed for it all the more.

After such pain, death, and destruction had claimed so many and so much, he'd ached for a proverbial sign from above. Through all his travel and his scavenging, he'd waited for it: a haloed figure descending unto him from a glorious dream; a soothing voice and its whisper of reassurance on the eastern wind; even, perchance, to see the heavens open up and grace him with a glimpse of the pearly gates swinging wide, revealing the face of God as He welcomed him home. At the very least, he longed for the Lord to touch his heart and fill it with that unshakeable faith he'd once known in his youth, before age and experience had scuffed and worn it, and long before the undead had taken everything else from him. He'd been waiting for something—anything—that showed his perseverance through the corpse of the world would be worth it.

What he was seeing now was certainly not that.

Before him sat the decrepit remains of what had once been the Church of the Holy Arms, at the edge of what had once been the town of Armistice, Tennessee. It would've been a modest yet charming place of worship before things went bad, but now, it was just a gutted and dirtied shell of its former self; another ghost in the graveyard. Most of its boards were missing (no doubt pilfered to barricade the homes he'd passed down the way), and those that weren't hung loosely about its two-story frame, chipped and stained from the elements of a bygone year. The dusty sign beside its front steps sported a line that Nathan knew to be from first Corinthians:

"Where, O death, is your victory? Where, O death, is your sting?"

Though Nathan found it to be abysmally ironic and just as haunting, it wasn't the verse that was giving him a chill in the midsummer heat; it was what hung in the church's lawn.

One of the Turned had been crucified there, suspended upon a large, crude cross driven into the dead grass. And it was still moving.

The thing was nude, save for a pair of tighty-whities that were now anything but white, the fabric stained by a mixture of blood, piss, shit, and the dirt of the days. The taut skin that covered its bones was just as filthy, the slowly decaying flesh covered in a coat of various grime, painting it a nauseous green-brown. It smelled even worse than it looked, the stench of its soiled self wafting Nathan's way from yards off. Its arms and legs were twig-slender, with what looked to be railroad spikes jammed through its wrists and overlapped ankles, hammered into the wood of the beams beneath. Its hands hung limply off to the sides, their fingers curling and uncurling lazily. The thing's torso was sickly thin; nothing but ribs. Long wisps of dark brown hair hung about its sunken and lightly-bearded face. Whoever he had been, he'd been in need of a trim and a shave by the time the apocalypse hit. Strands were blowing into its mouth as it turned and rolled its head about, wheezing feebly and jaws working as it chewed at the air.

It was a sad and awful sight. But what sickened Nathan the most to see was the small strand of Christmas lights that had been wrapped about the thing's brow, the tiny multicolored points jutting out all over across the scalp. It was no crown of thorns, but it was just as degrading.

Nathan was looking at a pseudo-Jesus Christ—undead, suffering, and hungry for flesh. The implication of it all was horrid, and the resemblance even more so.

To think that someone would have felt the need, much less found the time to erect this gross parody—even after the world had fallen to such turmoil and decay—was completely insane to Nathan. Never mind the blasphemy of it or whatever jaded religious critique might have inspired the deed; it was just plain wrong.

And, worse yet, Nathan realized that the Turned may not have been undead at the time it was nailed down and put up. One person could have done this to another—to the man who this creature had once been—and for whatever sick reason the aggressor may have thought justified it, leaving the man to Turn after a slow, agonizing death. Such cruelty certainly hadn't been beyond people of the past, and in far better times than the end of the world.

A memory came back to Nathan in that moment, crisp and complete.

It was of a time when he, Tara, and their daughter, Maddie, were at Sunday service. It'd been one of Maddie's first services, actually. At some point, his daughter had tugged at his sleeve while their priest was delivering his sermon. She'd had a worried look on her face, and Nathan had been hurt to see it. He'd leaned in and asked what was wrong; she'd pointed up to the giant bronze crucifix that hung over the priest's pulpit. In a whisper—and with all the concerned innocence that only a seven year old could have—she asked: "Why is that man hanging like that?"

Nathan had asked much the same of his mother and father when he'd been Maddie's age, and in that moment he'd told her exactly what they told him: "He did that for us. So that our sins would be forgiven by God. All of them. The ones we've done, and the ones we've yet to do." Maddie had seemed to accept this, and they'd gone back to listening to the service, holding each other's hand.

Another memory flashed to his mind after that—one of him holding his daughter's hand as she lay on the floor of what they'd thought was an abandoned home, her neck bleeding from the bite Tara had given her just before Nathan put his wife down, and before he'd have to do the same to his daughter so that she didn't Turn . . .

Nathan shoved the recollection aside as a throaty snarling caught his attention. He looked back up to the crucified Turned, which had finally caught sight of him. A little bit more life came into it as it leaned his way, its fingers wiggling excitedly, fighting to be free of the spikes and wanting to nibble on him.

The ones we've done, and the ones we've yet to do.

In this dead world full of dead people, Nathan thought there couldn't be many other bad things left for the living to do. This monument, or whatever the hell it could be called, showed otherwise. And he wasn't sure he could abide that.

Nathan glanced around, down either way of the country road and the tree lines about him. He listened intently for the slightest out-of-place noise. He neither saw nor heard anything that hinted of other Turned being nearby, and as he hadn't come across any in town, he figured the area was clear and safe. He could spare some time and his trusty hatchet and see to taking the crucifix down.

He closed the distance between himself and the hanging Turned, putting his shirt up over his nose to block the smell. It didn't do much good. His eyes had already started to water and the reek set him to coughing some. The Turned gave a sharp lunge as he stopped in front it, and he almost went for the Browning 1911-22 at his hip out of pure reaction. He stopped himself, though, knowing that a single shot could bring roaming Turned his way, if there did happen to be any about. Besides, he only had the one clip left and it was best to conserve it; plus, the Turned wasn't going anywhere. It was stuck fast to its crucifix and had no hope of getting at him. His hatchet could take care of it after he chopped down the cross.

He slid the hatchet out from his belt and set to hacking into the central beam. It was slower going than anticipated, but after a couple minutes of cutting away, the cross gave a tell-tale creak.

Nathan shoved his shoulder into the beam and brought it crashing down in a puff of kicked-up dirt, saving the Turned from having to land face first, though it may not have minded so much if it had. The undead didn't seem to pay much heed to pain. Case in point: when it landed, the Turned gave a nasty, angry shriek and started tugging violently away at its wrists. Nathan could hear its bones and its cartilage cracking and crunching from the harsh motion. The disgusting sound and that awful smell almost got Nathan to puke into his shirt, but he managed to hold it back.

Nathan scooted closer to the Turned and raised his hatchet over his head. He was about to bring it down and just finish the poor creature, but he stayed his hand. He lowered it, and while the thing kept on gnashing its teeth at him, he whispered a hurried prayer of Psalm 24.

He needed to do it. For the creature—for the person it used to be and the soul it used to have. For this world and whatever goodness must have remained within it. But most of all, he did it for himself. To remind him of his resolve, of all he had persevered, and all he would have to persevere in the days yet to come.

"The Lord is my shepherd; I shall not want. He maketh me to lie down in green pastures: he leadeth me beside the still waters. He restoreth my soul: he leadeth me in the paths of righteousness for his name's sake. Yea, though I walk through the valley of the shadow of death, I will fear no evil: for thou art with me; thy rod and thy staff they comfort me. Thou preparest a table before me in the presence of mine enemies: thou anointest my head with oil; my cup runneth over. Surely goodness and mercy shall follow me all the days of my life: and I will dwell in the house of the Lord forever. Amen."

With that, Nathan raised the hatchet again; as the Turned shot him a hateful glare, he brought the blade cutting straight down into its forehead. The thing's skull cracked open and the creature went still in an instant.

Nathan wrenched his weapon free, a stream of syrupy, dark blood seeping out from the Turned's head and coating the hatchet's edge. He delivered another dozen or so chops to the creature's wrists and ankles, severing them just above the steel spikes. When that was done, and the corpse had been freed of the beams, Nathan rolled it off and away from the cross.

He knelt there a moment, catching his breath as best he could and wiping his hatchet across the grass to clean it.

When he was rested, he returned the weapon to his side and hauled himself up. He'd leave the corpse where it lay; that it was freed of the cross was enough courtesy for both of them. Sparing it and the Church of the Holy Arms one last glance, Nathan turned and kept on with his trek.

He figured he'd keep on following the road west and just see where it led him. He hoped wherever that was, it just might hold that sign he'd so desperately hoped for. Stepping off the lawn and back on to gravel, he kept his eyes to the road, his heart on God, and his hopes reaching towards heaven.

He wasn't on the road for more than five minutes—just barely out of the city limits—when two of the Turned came running at him from the trees, biting and tearing away at him before he could pull his gun or brandish a prayer.

About the Author

Patrick Winters is a graduate of Illinois College in Jacksonville, IL, where he earned a Bachelor of Arts degree in English Literature and Creative Writing. As a student, he was a member of the international English honors society, Sigma Tau Delta.

Winters is an avid listener of all things hard-rock and heavy-metal, a compendium of comic-book knowledge, can (and will) do a perplexing array of voice impersonations, and can bend his thumbs further back than any person should have the right/capability of doing. It is all quite odd . . .

Website:
http://wintersauthor.azurewebsites.net/Pages/Welcome